Gordon Christopher Beaulieu, M.D.

Prescription for taking Savanah:

1. Mix equal parts honesty and charm—as needed.

2. Double the recommended daily allowance of tenderness—to be applied liberally.

3. Megadoses of passionate kisses—administered every chance I get.

Signed *[signature]* M.D.

Please address questions and book requests to: Silhouette Reader Service
U.S.: 3010 Walden Ave., P.O. Box 1325, Buffalo, NY 14269
Canadian: P.O. Box 609, Fort Erie, Ont. L2A 5X3

Solution: Wedding

PEPPER ADAMS
TAKING SAVANAH

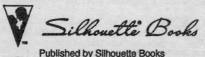

Published by Silhouette Books
America's Publisher of Contemporary Romance

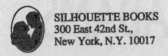 **SILHOUETTE BOOKS**
300 East 42nd St.,
New York, N.Y. 10017

ISBN 0-373-30148-0

TAKING SAVANAH

Copyright © 1988 by Debrah Morris and Pat Shaver

Celebrity Wedding Certificates published by permission of
Donald Ray Pounders from *Celebrity Wedding Ceremonies*.

This edition published by arrangement with Harlequin Books S.A.

® and TM are trademarks of Harlequin Books S.A., used under license.
Trademarks indicated with ® are registered in the United States Patent and
Trademark Office, the Canadian Trade Marks Office and in other countries.

Printed in U.S.A.

A Letter from the Author

Dear Reader,

Taking Savanah was our third novel for Silhouette Romance and was published early in our career. It was inspired by the romantic comedies of the thirties and forties we both loved to watch on the late show when we were growing up. Our goal was to combine two popular themes in one story—the marriage of convenience and the secret child.

We also included the concepts of family commitment and love the second time around, as well as the dynamics of a doctor-and-nurse relationship. This was a tall order, but our efforts seemed to appeal to the editors of Silhouette and, most important, to you, our readers. Thank you.

Our story takes place in the South. To us, the area conjures visions of mint juleps on the veranda, warm moonlit nights and the heady scent of magnolias and peach blossoms. We've added a dash of the fierce regional pride of the Southerners who maintain an historical wariness of anyone from "up North." We've also spiced it up by blending in a passionate love that could never die, and the result is *Taking Savanah*.

As one would say in Georgia, we're "just plumb tickled pink" that Silhouette has chosen to reissue *Taking Savanah*. And we sincerely hope you feel the same way, too.

Pepper Adams

With special thanks to Aunt Bennie
and my nephew Tim

Chapter One

"I'm looking for Savanah Winslow," Gordon Beaulieu called to the little boy, who was idly pushing a wooden car across the veranda steps. When the child looked up at the sound of Beau's voice, Beau leaned across his convertible's seat. "Does she live here?"

The child nodded, but didn't take his eyes off Beau's low-slung red car. He was obviously more interested in it than in answering questions.

Satisfied that he'd finally reached his destination, Beau pulled the Mercedes into the shade of a huge magnolia tree, switched off the engine, and got out. He pressed his fists to the small of his back and enjoyed stretching his long frame after so many hours on the road. The car was long on speed and pizzazz, but halfway between Boston and Harmony, Georgia, Beau wished he'd indentured himself for the full-size luxury model.

He stood for a moment, surveying his surroundings, appreciating the Norman Rockwell-like setting. The early evening quiet, broken only by the buzz of insects and the clickety-clack of a manual mower being pushed across a nearby lawn, was foreign to his city-bred ears.

Although it was early April, and the first signs of spring were just beginning to show in Boston, Mother Nature had already visited her bounty on the more hospitable climate of Harmony. Forsythia banked the gracious old homes with clouds of brilliant yellow, and tulips and narcissus splashed their bright colors on already green lawns.

Comparing the quaint serenity of Savanah's hometown with the restless animation of his own, Beau let himself through the old-fashioned white picket gate and sauntered up the flower-bordered walk to the house. No one was about except the little boy. "Anyone home?"

The boy nodded again, pushing back a stray lock of sandy-brown hair with a small, unboyishly clean hand.

Beau didn't have much personal experience with children, but as a doctor who'd done more than one rotation through pediatrics, he judged the child to be approximately five years old. Surely old enough to talk. He tried again. "Anyone besides you?"

He should have seen it coming. The boy's dark blue eyes focused on him thoughtfully, and he answered with another nod, more energetic now that the novelty of the car had worn off.

"Anyone who can talk?" he joked, hoping to conceal the exasperation he felt.

The child giggled behind his hands, nodding again.

What should have been a simple encounter had degenerated into a game, and Beau tried to recall how many of the traditional twenty questions he'd already used. Stepping up the veranda, he sat down on the top step and leaned back on his elbows. Smiling gently, he tried a different approach, a question that couldn't be answered with a nod. "Why aren't you talking to me?"

"'Cause I'm not 'sposed to talk to strangers," the lad confided matter-of-factly, in speech totally devoid of *r*s.

Beau grinned. "That's a good policy, but I'm not a stranger. I know Savanah Winslow. Do you?"

"Sure."

Before he had a chance to pursue the matter, the screen door opened and an elderly woman wearing bifocals and a pompadour of white hair stepped out. Her pale skin stretched softly over fragile bones and Beau recognized Great-Aunt Jasmine immediately on the basis of Savanah's long-ago description.

He recalled that the elderly belle had never married and wondered how the local swains had resisted. The petulant beauty of her youth was still very apparent in her aged face. She had to be nearly eighty, he estimated, but there was a frisky spryness to her step and demeanor.

She stooped slightly, giving the impression of having shrunk inside the shapeless print dress that hung in folds over her nonexistent bosom. A gingham apron was tied at her narrow waist. She wore rolled-down stockings and no-nonsense white oxfords.

She stepped between Beau and the child protectively and, tugging a lace-edged handkerchief from her apron pocket, fanned herself in a harried manner. "Might I be of some little help to you, sir?" she asked in a soft drawl reminiscent of violets and cotillions. The softness couldn't conceal a lively inquisitiveness.

"I hope so." He extended his hand in greeting. "I'm Gordon Christopher Beaulieu." He paused to see what reaction his name would produce, but when it resulted in no more than pleasant curiosity, he went on.

"The man at the gas station told me Savanah Winslow lived here."

"I'm Jasmine Jefferson, Savanah's aunt." She took his hand and shook it delicately. "Was the man you spoke to a long drink of water in disgraceful coveralls?"

Beau smiled at the apt description and nodded.

"Must have been Cletus Tyrell. He's a one-man information center. Self-appointed, you understand."

"Of course," he answered absently, wondering why his name wasn't familiar to Savanah's aunt. Had the old lady forgotten, or hadn't his former wife ever told her family about their whirlwind courtship, hasty elopement and subsequent annulment? "I'm an old...um...college friend of Savanah's and just happened to be in this part of the country. I'd like to see her. Is she home?"

Jasmine peered over her bifocals in an attempt to read the M.D. plates on his car. "She will be directly. And you'd be from—where, Dr. Beaulieu?"

"Boston." She'd seen through his lame excuse about just being in the neighborhood, but he hoped she was too well-bred to call him out on it.

"Boston? Why, you've come a far piece to see our little Savanah. I do hope you'll stay for supper." Before he could reply, she turned to the boy. "Kit, run and tell Pippy we have a guest and ask her to set another place at the table."

To Beau she continued breathlessly, "We always have Doc Ashburton, Savanah's employer, over for Friday night supper, you see, and with you here it'll almost be like a party. It's been ever so long since we had a party. You will stay, won't you?"

Southern hospitality in action. Her tone said it would be a breach of etiquette to refuse, but Beau felt a little guilty about misleading the woman. Once they found out why he was here, he'd be lucky if they didn't tar and feather him. "I don't want to impose—"

"Fiddlesticks. Any friend of Savanah's is more than welcome. I'm sure she'll just be tickled pink to see you again after so long."

He wasn't so sure of that. Considering the terms on which they'd parted over five and a half years before, it was entirely possible she'd throw him out on his Yankee butt. He should have telephoned to let her know he was coming, but she would have hung up on him or, at the very least, demanded he state his business. The news he'd brought was best delivered in person, preferably with the recipient sitting down.

No doubt his unexpected appearance would be a shock, but there wasn't much point in putting off the reunion, or confrontation as it might turn out to be, much longer. "Thank you, Miss Jefferson, I appreciate your kindness. I've been eating road food for a couple of days now."

Jasmine led the way into the parlor and they were joined by her younger, but not by much, sister. Savanah's grandmother, Phillipa Jane Potter, was a whittled down version of the flighty Jasmine. The sisters were nothing alike in temperament and it soon became apparent that while Pippy was suspicious of outsiders in general, Yankees required special scrutiny.

"More peach brandy, Doctor?" Jasmine hovered at the arm of Beau's chair like a manic hummingbird, her agitated movements threatening the fragile bric-a-brac that decorated the room.

"No, thank you." Beau covered the red-stemmed cordial glass with one hand in case the old dear wouldn't take his word for it. He was a Scotch-on-the-rocks man and had only downed the sweet viscous liqueur to be courteous.

"Very well, then." Jasmine's wrinkled face trembled, then she affected a look of affronted resignation. She retreated to a spindly chair and perched anxiously on the needlepoint seat, ready for action should he come to his senses and change his mind.

His other hostess harrumphed her disapproval from a violently red settee abloom with antimacassars. "Sister and I make it ourselves, you know," Phillipa Jane sniffed. "From an old and treasured family recipe. Jefferson peach brandy was good enough for General Lee, but apparently *some people* don't know a good thing when they taste it."

Beau winced at the obvious rebuff. He should try to make a few points with the two ladies and win their favor before they realized who he was and the shouting began. He was botching the job. Even his refusal of a refill violated some unwritten code of Southern etiquette. He mentally calculated the number of faux pas he'd already committed and offered a watered-down version of his patented grin.

"And a finer brandy I've never tasted, Mrs. Potter," he perjured himself. "I'm just not that much of a drinker." Not of sugar straight up, anyway. This waiting was beginning to get to him, and he longed for a stiff shot of just about anything else.

"Just call her Pippy," Jasmine urged. "Everybody does."

Beau glanced at her for consent, and her thin lips made what might have been a smile, but it was hard to tell. It could easily have been a thinly disguised snarl.

The ensuing silence was broken only by the determined ticking of the grandfather clock. The last of the diluted sunlight had long since filtered through the heavy lace curtains, and Jasmine switched on a Tiffany lamp, which created a puddle of greenish light on the Oriental carpet.

Beau reached up to loosen his tie, and remembered, too late, that he wasn't wearing one. He should have worn something more formal than a cotton sweater and jeans. He mentally added appropriate attire to his growing list of social crimes.

The watchful eyes of the aged sisters made him nervous, and he searched his nearly depleted reserve of small talk for something to say. They'd already covered the weather, concluding it was unseasonably warm. The ladies asked polite questions about his family, their refined drawls making his clipped New England answers sound harsh and uncouth, even to his own ears.

Their matched sets of white eyebrows elevated, and Jasmine's hand fluttered to her chest when he divulged the information that his parents were divorced, and he'd been reared by his mother "up north." Just as he'd guessed, non-Southerners and their motives were clearly suspect.

Though being a Yankee was a mark against him, Beau felt he won points by mentioning that his father was a native Georgian. Beau had taken his medical degree at Emory, where he'd met Savanah. Then he promptly lost them by admitting he'd returned to Boston to do his internship and residency.

By his computation, his northeastern background and the brandy blunder placed him on the negative end of the favor scale. The ladies would probably go into vapor lock when they found out his real reason for coming to Harmony. It was obvious they knew nothing of his past relationship with Savanah and he let them believe, temporarily, that they'd become acquainted while she was in nursing school.

Actually that much was true. While he wasn't guilty of outright lying, he'd sinned by omission by not disabusing them of their false assumptions. It was strange that Savanah had kept their brief marriage and annulment such a deep, dark secret.

Then again, he didn't understand a lot of the things she'd done—like walking out on him after a scorching honeymoon that had proved the old adage about the attraction of opposites. After the dust had settled in their small garage apartment, they realized they were virtual strangers and were overwhelmed by the enormousness of what they'd done. Maybe they could have worked out their differences, but there hadn't been time. Scarcely three weeks elapsed between their first heated meeting and their chilly farewell in an Atlanta attorney's office. That had to be a record even in these uncertain times.

"Tell us, Dr. Beaulieu," Jasmine piped into Beau's rambling thoughts. "Whatever are you doing in our little corner of the world?" She had pulled the dainty handkerchief from her apron pocket and waved it to attract his attention.

Beau shifted in his seat and stalled for time. This would be tricky. The whole truth and nothing but the truth was out of the question for the time being, but a variation thereof might work. "I've just finished my residency and have decided to take a break from the pressure. I've always liked Georgia and thought a nice driving vacation would be just what the doctor ordered, so to speak."

Jasmine tittered, but Pippy scowled. "How well do you know our Savanah?" questioned the latter, cutting right to the heart of the matter. She glared at him as though trying to recall if she'd seen his picture in the post office recently.

"Fairly well, actually," he evaded. "Though we haven't kept in touch over the past few years."

"Now, isn't that just too bad?" Jasmine asked no one in particular.

"Pardon me for saying so," Pippy remarked thoughtfully. "But you don't look old enough to be a doctor. I daresay I have drawers older'n you."

"Oh, sister," Jasmine reprimanded with a flutter. "You've got drawers older'n abolition."

"I swan, Jasmine!" Pippy shook her head dismissively. "We may be old, but we're not that old."

"Just a figure of speech, sister. And of course he's a doctor, his license plate says so."

The clock ticked ominously, minutes passed.

Jasmine chose to fill the silence with stories of Savanah's heroic commitment to duty. The tales jibed perfectly with Beau's memories of her as a serious, hardworking young woman who'd managed to finish nursing school with her idealism intact.

It disconcerted Beau to talk about Savanah, to get a glimpse of the woman she'd become. He had known more about her physical needs than her career ambitions, having spent most of their short acquaintance introducing her to the wonders of loving. She'd been an apt pupil in the subject and eager to both learn and please. He'd been touched by her innocence and had reveled in the joy she'd found in her newly awakened passion. Recalling the intense feelings they'd shared made him suddenly wonder if that fire could ever be rekindled.

Sweet memories of their brief happiness lingered, undiminished by the years. Those thoughts had survived along with the never-quite-forgotten pain of losing her. Beau reminded himself why he'd come here in the first place and tried to put the old memories in their proper place.

Eventually, Pippy left to inspect the progress of dinner, and returned with the little boy in tow. "I believe you've already met our Kit, Savanah's son."

Savanah's son? The words nearly jolted Beau out of his chair. He'd wondered about Kit earlier but had assumed he belonged to a neighbor. How could Savanah have a child? Dumb question for a doctor, he thought before answering himself. In the usual manner, you fool. But who was the little guy's father? More importantly, *where* was he?

It had never occurred to Beau that Savanah might have remarried and had a family by now, but he should have realized someone like Savanah wouldn't stay unattached for long. However, it was damned difficult to think of another man being on the receiving end of that passionate nature. Ego, pure and simple, had made Beau ignore the possibility of anyone replacing him.

Then Beau calmed down. Savanah wasn't married or she wouldn't be known as Winslow. Perhaps she hadn't married again at all, but either way there had been another man in her life. That thought caused him to sit up a little straighter. She was really going to love his news! he thought sarcastically.

Forcing those ideas out of his head, he looked closely at the child and contemplated how it must feel to be counted among the old ladies' possessions as the little man extended his right hand. "Hello again, sir." Only it sounded like "suh" when he said it.

"How're you doin' sport?" Noting the child's portrait-perfect appearance, Beau wondered if the poor kid was ever allowed to get dirty. He reminded himself that it was none of his business. He'd given up the right to interfere in Savanah's life, and therefore her child's, years before.

He was a fine-looking boy, his large blue eyes a replica of his mother's. Beau felt drawn to the child and wondered if it was because he, too, had been reared in a houseful of women. The boy's manners were impeccable, but it troubled Beau that he was so... so neat.

Kit seated himself gingerly on the settee, careful to keep his shoes off the cushions, and folded his hands in his lap in a very unchildlike manner. Beau empathized with the kid's reverential attitude, the funeral parlor ambience of the house positively inspired it.

He should be outside playing with his friends. His shoes scuffed and tied with broken laces, his jeans sporting holes in the knees, not knife-edge creases. He should smell of puppies and peanut butter, not Pear's soap. By way of conversation, he asked, "Do you play baseball, Kit?"

"No, sir." Unlike his Aunt Jasmine, Kit wasn't one to waste his breath on idle chatter.

"Football?"

Kit shook his head. "I'm too little."

"Do you swim?"

"Not yet. Granny Pip wants me to wait 'til I'm this many," he divulged, waving six baby fingers. His sturdy little body wiggled. "I gots a Nerf basketball in my room, and a critter cage in the garage."

Good news at last. Beau was relieved the kid had some natural aptitude for snips and snails. "What kind of critters? Hamsters?"

"No, sir. Gosh!" A look of amused astonishment stole over the boy's delicate features, and he giggled behind splayed fingers. "Hamsters have babies and make messes and smell to high heaven."

Beau's mind flashed a picture of Pippy and Jasmine hard at work for the CIA, brainwashing division. "I never thought of that." And neither should a little kid.

Kit shrugged. " 'Sides, my critter cage is real little. Doc made it outta an old window screen." He brightened. "I got two crickets in there right now."

Crickets? The all-American boy's starter set. "Maybe you could show them to me sometime."

"Sure. Last summer, Doc taught me how to catch lightning bugs. But they died."

"They will." It was difficult to find common ground with a boy who required lessons in bug catching, but Beau longed to take him in hand and teach him the rowdy joys of boyhood.

"I do believe we should go ahead with our supper before it's ruined,' Pippy announced. "Perhaps Savanah and Doc got held up at the clinic. I could just totter across the street and check on them, but they should be here soon. Kit, dear, go wash up."

The ladies departed for the fragrant kitchen. Beau followed Kit into the foyer, watching him mount the stairs. He couldn't help wondering why such a spick-and-span kid needed to wash.

Alone, he glanced at the family portraits on the wall and found several of Savanah. There was no mistaking the dark ringlets of the wide-eyed toddler, or the gap-toothed child, or the happy teenager in a baton twirler's outfit, and he instantly recognized her as the proud graduate.

He stared at the portrait, remembering. Dark curls tumbled from her starched nurse's cap, and he recalled her claiming her unruly hair was the bane of her existence. He'd kissed her neck and ran his fingers through it, assuring her she had sexy hair. She'd laughed self-consciously and kissed him back.

"That's my mommy, isn't she pretty?" Kit asked as he came downstairs, one small hand skimming the wide banister.

"You have a beautiful mom, sport."

"I know," he agreed. "We better go in to supper now."

"I suppose so." Beau moved closer to the sedate, too-old little boy. An overwhelming urge to see him act like a normal kid prompted him to whisper conspiratorially, "Have you ever slid down this banister?"

Kit's eyes widened with childish surprise that an adult would suggest such a thing. "Nope," he admitted, "but I thought about it. I'd probably get in big trouble if I did."

"Probably." If those two old ladies had anything to say about it, the poor kid would be crocheting doilies by puberty.

The boy eyed the banister with a gleeful expression and his mouth slowly stretched into a wide smile. "Have you?"

"Ever slid down a banister? Sure, lots of times. We had one just like it when I was a boy."

Kit glanced nervously at the doorway before whispering, "Hey, wanna show me how?"

The notion of corrupting such a clean slate was too tempting; and before he had time to consider what rules of conduct he might be violating, Beau mounted the stairs at a fast clip. At the top, he threw his left leg over the wide glossy rail and counted down from ten for effect.

When he reached zero, Kit's enthusiastic "Blast off!" sent Beau plummeting, backside first, down its length. He felt the warm friction on the seat of his pants and experienced the same thrilling breathlessness he remembered from childhood. However, time had somewhat clouded the memory of the pain and he soon regretted his impulsive action.

Unmanning himself was hardly the example he wanted to set. The ride was over sooner than he expected and, instead of the dignified light-as-air landing he'd planned, he found himself suddenly, and momentarily, airborne. The free-floating sensation ended on impact.

His next perception was that of lying sprawled, in a most embarrassing way, atop a soft warm body. He knew it wasn't Kit's by the enticingly feminine fragrance it gave off. He remembered that perfume. It was a wildly intimate scent, hinting of magnolias and sultry Southern nights.

Beau rolled to his side and stared into familiar, startlingly blue eyes, so outstanding amid the tangle of raven-wing lashes and brows. Memory hadn't been entirely infallible; he'd forgotten how arresting Savanah's face actually was.

Her nose was tweakably tilted and below it her mouth was as full and kissable as he recalled. He noted that it was presently set in a grim line which emphasized the graceful thrust of her jaw. He fought the impulse to draw his finger along the subtle sweep of cheekbones, to feel once again her soft honey-colored skin.

He saw in her face everything he remembered loving: honesty, resilience and intelligence. But maturity had left its mark, for now there was a sad knowledge in her eyes, along with other emotions he couldn't name at the moment.

The lady was definitely surprised. It wasn't every day a former husband came hurtling down from above to knock her senseless on the foyer floor. Her look of astonishment was gone in a heartbeat, replaced by passionate anger of thunderous proportions.

"It's you!" she shrieked, knowing her shock was apparent to everyone within earshot. Despite the strange car in the driveway, Gordon Christopher Beaulieu III was the last person on earth she'd expected to see when she'd stepped into the house. An incompatible combination of anger and delight made her gasp, and the power of her reaction made her long for a paper bag into which she could breathe.

"It is indeed." He propped himself up on one elbow and looked down at her. While their reunion had a certain charm, it wasn't how he visualized the moment.

Savanah was a nurse and recognized the unmistakable symptoms of adrenaline overload: pounding heart, racing pulse, dizziness. And she had them all. She opened her mouth to speak, but changed her mind. No self-respecting mother would utter, in front of her child, the words that trembled on her tongue.

"You don't seem very happy to see me," Beau said.

Happy to see him? For years she'd longed to know, just once more, the sheer breath-stealing nearness of him, to experience his proud masculine perfection and special brand of loving. She'd fantasized about seeing him again and wondered if he'd still have the same leveling impact on her, if he could still reduce her to a quivering puddle of need. Now she knew.

She'd finally gotten to the point where she didn't think about him all the time. Whole days sometimes went by without one painful memory thrusting itself into her consciousness. She'd faced down the small-town gossip regarding her husband's secret identity and kept her head up throughout her pregnancy.

She'd fought for both her's and Kit's acceptance in a community where family trees were the official plant. She could have avoided such problems by leaving, but she hadn't. She'd stayed because Harmony was her home, the only one she'd ever known. Beau's sudden, unwelcome appearance would be like waving a red flag in front of gossips' noses and could very well tear down the fragile house of cards she'd built of her life.

Why had he come? And why did he have to look so good? Damn his faultless skin. Damn his hair that was even more sun-streaked and curly than she remembered. Damn his deep, brown eyes and their crinkly amusement.

She wasn't the same naive girl who'd eloped in a fury of hot passion and lived to regret it. The loneliness and pain of the past few years had tempered her, forging a new strength that would help her resist the temptation of Gordon Beaulieu.

She'd changed, but he still seemed the same. What did he want? What had prompted his sudden appearance in Harmony? She stopped interrogating herself and addressed her questions to the one person who could answer them.

"What are you doing here?" she squeaked in a tone that clearly indicated she might be afraid to hear the answer.

"Having supper?" he ventured with a familiar grin.

"Here? In this house? Who on God's green earth invited you?"

Kit struggled to his feet from the floor where he'd collapsed in a fit of giggles. "Granny Pip and Auntie Jasmine invited him, Mommy. Say hey to Dr. Beaulieu."

"Why would they do such a crazy thing?" She knew her words were tinged with hysteria, but she couldn't help it. A quick look at Kit told her he was confused by her panic and hostility. Hoping explanations wouldn't be necessary later, she said, "Kit, go see if Granny Pip needs any help." Then she turned her wrath on Beau. "I don't know what ever possessed them, but..."

He waited until Kit had scampered away. "Evidently, they've been blessed with more Southern hospitality than you. They took pity on a road-weary traveler and invited me to stay for dinner."

"Over my dead body," she whispered before realizing the irony of her words. He was already over her body, and it was not dead. Not by a long shot. Every point where his warm skin touched hers tingled with a wistful excitement. "If you don't mind," she ground out in a frosty tone, "I'd like to get up now."

He clambered to his feet. "Sure thing. I think we're getting ahead of ourselves, anyway," he whispered suggestively, extending a hand to pull her up. Savanah hesitated before taking it. He had that just-trust-me look on his face and she remembered so well what could happen when she did. She rubbed her posterior gingerly where it had thudded heavily to the floor.

"I didn't hurt you, did I?" He hadn't expected her to be so hostile. Surprise and a little anger at his sudden appearance would've been understandable, but he'd immodestly assumed once the shock of seeing him again had worn off, she'd be delighted. That furrow between her brows did not indicate delight.

"No." Her voice had transcended frosty and would now freeze alcohol at fifty paces. It was an innocent enough question, she told herself. It had nothing to do with the five and a half years of missing him, wondering if she'd made the right decision.

Allowing him to pull her to her feet was a mistake. His touch brought long-repressed emotions whirling to life, and her hand trembled in his before she jerked it away. The heat rushed to her face and her heart threatened cardiac arrest. Lord, he could still do it to her and she was a fool to let him.

"What are you doing in Harmony?" she shouted quietly.

"I came to see you."

"See me? Now? All these years without so much as a word, and all of a sudden you've come to see me? I want the truth, Beau. Now."

"I'm trying to tell you," he said calmly. "If you'll only stop shrieking."

"I am not—" she began, then consciously lowered her voice and glanced toward the kitchen. "I am not shrieking. Why are you here?"

"Something's come up that you need to know about."

Savanah shook her head to clear it of tumbling thoughts.

"And just what is so monumentally important that *you'd* drive almost a thousand miles to tell me?"

"Maybe you should sit down. The news may be a bit unnerving." He took her elbow to guide her to a nearby chair, but she yanked way from him.

"I do not need to sit down. And I do not want to sit down. Just tell me what you came here to say and get out." Her eyes widened. "Do Pippy and Jasmine know who you—"

"Your secret is safe, Savanah. Though, I confess I'm a little confused that you chose not to tell them about me."

There were things she hadn't told them and not knowing had hurt them terribly. "Why did you come here, Beau?"

"To tell you that our annulment was never filed." Grasping her shoulders when she swayed on her feet, he looked deeply into her wide, frightened eyes and made their position perfectly clear. "In the eyes of the law, Savanah, we're still man and wife."

Chapter Two

"No." Her voice was a breathless whisper. "That can't be. It's impossible."

Beau felt the heat of her skin through the lightweight fabric of her nurse's uniform. "Inconvenient, maybe. Unfortunate and implausible, yes. But it's definitely possible." He nearly obeyed the silent command which pulled his lips toward hers, but the stunned, unhappy look in her eyes made him withdraw at the last moment.

They stood a hairbreadth apart. She was stunned by the implications of his words and both of them were buffeted by memories, unable to break the spell spinning around them. But Jasmine, calling them in to supper, had no such problem and her appearance in the doorway precluded further discussion. "I see you two have had your little reunion. Why, Savanah, dear, you're white as a bedsheet. Are you all right?"

"Fine. I'm fine." Fine? She'd never be fine again. Her world was tumbling down around her, and her life would never be the same. She'd just learned she was still married and couldn't demand an explanation or even cry in frustration. She had to act as if nothing were wrong until she could get Beau alone and question him at length about his preposterous story.

They needed privacy after Beau's little bombshell, but the small foyer was suddenly crowded. Doc Ashburton arrived and was duly introduced. Then Kit was sent by Pippy to tell everyone supper was getting cold.

Reluctantly, Savanah took her place at the table beside Kit, certain she'd never make it through the meal. She glanced around her son, catching Beau's consuming gaze from the other side. He exuded an infuriating calm that made her want to slap his handsome face. No doubt he'd come to tie up whatever legal loose ends had been left dangling years before by obtaining her signature on a piece of paper. All she had to do was give him what he wanted, and he'd be on his way before he could begin asking dangerous questions.

For the first time she became aware of the rapport that had apparently developed between Beau and Kit. Her son was gazing at Beau as if he'd never heard a man talk before, and Savanah recognized the signs of incipient hero worship. That would be disastrous. As much as Kit needed a male role model, it simply could not be Beau. Not at this late date.

Living in a household of women, Kit was sure to miss something. Having no masculine influence hadn't been such a big problem when he was an infant and toddler, but now that he was growing up, Savanah worried that there was no one to teach him all the little things men traditionally taught small boys. Dear old Doc did his best, but he simply wasn't capable of keeping up with Kit's boundless energy.

Savanah tried to be both mother and father, but it was growing harder every day. Her job at the clinic kept her away for long hours. The love Pippy and Jasmine lavished on Kit compensated for most of their unprogressive short-comings, but lately Savanah had noticed they were squelching his normal boyish enthusiasm by pressing upon him their own outdated ideas and rules of conduct.

Kit stood to lose the most in the untidy situation, and she couldn't allow him to form any emotional attachments to Beau. Not only that, but if Beau learned that the child whose hair he was absently ruffling was his own flesh and blood, it would mean the end of life as she knew it.

The meal was torture. Every time she opened her mouth to pop in a bit of mashed potato or fried chicken, harsh recriminations trembled on her tongue like a gang of convicts primed for the big break. She had to clamp down more than once to avoid saying something she'd regret.

As she watched Beau ply his trademark charm on Pippy and Jasmine, she wondered what their reaction would be if she told them he was Kit's heretofore unidentified father. That little tidbit would initiate a few swooning sessions.

Despite all she had to worry about, Savanah understood the folly of letting Pippy and Jasmine in on the truth. Next to bingo, finding a husband for her and a father for Kit was their favorite pastime. To have both practically handed to them on a silver platter would create emotional chaos.

They had their hearts set on a June wedding in the gazebo and moped around the house each year that month came and went. If they ever found out the truth, they wouldn't rest until the matrimonial knots were retied and family unity restored.

She'd informed Pippy and Jasmine of her brief marriage and its subsequent annulment when she'd returned home. But, as a matter of pride, she'd steadfastly refused to divulge her husband's name in order to avoid their well-meaning interference. By the time her pregnancy became apparent, Savanah was glad she'd kept the name of her husband to herself.

For weeks they'd begged to be enlightened, arguing that a man had a right to know he was about to become a father. They insisted the town gossips would ease up when they saw he was real and not a fabrication as some already suspected. But Savanah had remained firm. Everything surrounding her relationship with Beau was too personal and painful.

The gossipmongers didn't bother her so much. While they were talking about her unexpected pregnancy, they were giving some other poor soul a rest. So the good citizens of Harmony were left to think what they would, and their imaginations hadn't failed them.

She watched Beau surreptitiously and some of her panic subsided. Surely, he didn't suspect Kit's paternity. If he did he wouldn't be calmly buttering a biscuit and discussing the latest surgical procedures with

Doc. How it had escaped his notice, she couldn't fathom.

Why didn't he realize Kit was his son? It was written all over their faces, that similar something in their bone structures, the unmistakable sameness of their lopsided grins, their look-alike dimples. Kit was a chip off the Beaulieu block, and she crossed her fingers under the table and prayed no one else would put two and two together.

It was the strangest meal Beau ever sat through. Every time he glanced in Savanah's direction, she wore a different expression. He'd noted everything from distress to determination to what he hoped wasn't disdain. It was unfortunate that he hadn't broken the news to her more gently, choosing a moment when he could have explained how their sticky situation had occurred. Her reaction stung him. Was being his wife really so terrible? Obviously she thought so.

"More chicken, Dr. Beau?" Jasmine offered him the platter. Her familiar form of address let everyone know the young doctor had won her personal approval.

"No, thank you," he protested when he realized he'd already consumed more than his share. "I couldn't eat another bite."

Thank goodness. Savanah could barely maintain an air of strained civility, but Beau was actually enjoying himself. The next time he winked at her on the sly, she was going to haul off and kick him in the shin. She couldn't wait to get him alone and lambast him for subjecting her to such an ordeal.

"Peach cobbler?" Pippy tempted. "With cream?"

"He *said* he was full," Savanah muttered. What he was *full* of would fertilize every field in the area. It was disgusting the way he'd impressed Doc and charmed the two innocent old ladies. Even the uncharmable Pippy was pressing her precious cobbler on him.

Beau hadn't exactly expected Savanah to welcome him with open arms, but such icy hostility was more than he could bear. She was more cynical than he remembered, and a hell of a lot more beautiful. He liked her hair short, its disarray gave her an air of having just been tumbled out of bed. The lushness of the curves under that pristinely white uniform were those of a sensual woman. As soon as he got her alone again, he intended to kiss that self-righteous look right off her face.

"Cobbler?" Beau winked at Kit. "We men like our desserts even better than dinner, don't we, son?"

Savanah's chest ached, and she winced at the unconsciously appropriate form of address.

Kit nodded vigorously. "Yes, sir. We surely do."

"Eat the rest of your vegetables first," she reminded him automatically. "You know the rules."

"Yes'm," the child mumbled.

"And Kit, dear," Pippy added. "It's bad manners to speak with your mouth full."

"I'd better clean up my plate, too." Beau speared a green bean peevishly. Kit's obedient acquiescence to so many rules disturbed him, and he didn't know why.

"Where are you planning to stay while you're visiting?" Doc asked between bites of cobbler.

"He's just passing through and won't be staying. Will you?" Savanah leveled Beau a look that made it perfectly clear the town wasn't big enough for both of them.

He'd almost forgotten how damnably attractive she was when she got up on her Southern high horse. Those old feelings were back, stronger than ever. From the moment he'd laid eyes on her, his motivations for coming had begun to change. Just to make sure the old fire was out for good, he'd like nothing better than to get her back in bed just once. Well, maybe twice to be absolutely certain. "Actually I thought I might hang around a while."

Savanah spluttered in her iced tea. "You can't be serious?"

"Why not? Harmony's a nice change of pace. I'm a little disillusioned with my life-style in Boston." Not only that, but it simply wasn't as satisfying as it should be. "I don't like my credibility as a surgeon confused with my ability to play good host or my acceptability as a party guest."

"For someone with your athletic ability," Savanah chided, "a sport like social climbing shouldn't pose any problems."

He gave her a touché nod. "Doc's been singing the praises of family medicine and his life here. I'd like to see firsthand what the life of a country doctor is really like." In reality, it wasn't so much small-town living that intrigued him, but Savanah. "That is, if Doc doesn't mind."

"Mind? I'd be pleased as punch to show you around." Doc pushed his glasses up on his balding head and leaned away from the table to make room for his full round belly.

"In that case, I may just stick around for a while."
Beau surprised himself with the sudden decision.

"You won't like it here," Savanah assured him.
"There's no theaters, nightclubs or five-star restaurants. No bright lights. You'll be bored to death inside a week."

"People change," he said meaningfully.

"Not that much, they don't."

"Well, young fella," Doc said expansively, "if you do stay over, why don't you bunk at my place across the street? I've plenty of room even with the clinic taking up one wing of the house. The only motel in town is way out on the highway and my spare room is more comfortable than Doolittle's boarding house. It would give you a chance to see how a small-town medical office works."

Beau didn't stop to consider what he was getting into. For some reason, he'd made up his mind to accept Doc's offer before he'd finished making it. "I'd be happy to accept your hospitality, sir."

Savanah glared at the two of them, not sure which one she would throttle first.

"Nothing's free in this life, boy," Doc said with a laugh. "I reckon you won't mind being on call while I'm gone?"

"Of course not. I'd be happy to help out."

Savanah had forgotten Doc's fishing trip and panicked at the thought of working alongside Beau. "But you already made arrangements with a doctor over in Warm Springs."

"I know, but he's got his own duties and it would be a shame to waste the talents of a bright young fella like Beau. Can't get any of those young hotshots to come to small towns these days, they want to stay in the cities where the big money is. Maybe if we make Beau feel welcome, we can prevail upon him to move here and hang out his shingle.''

"Now wouldn't that be nice?'' cooed Jasmine.

"Wouldn't it just?'' Savanah didn't like the way things were developing.

"I need to start planning for my retirement, I ain't getting any younger,'' Doc continued. "It would be comforting to have someone in line to take up the torch, so to speak.''

"And wouldn't it be nice for Savanah to work with an old friend?'' asked Pippy with an uncharacteristic display of tolerance.

Savanah shot Beau another fierce look when he grinned and said, "Wouldn't it just?''

The table was cleared and Doc and the ladies left for their Friday-night bingo game, saying Savanah and Beau must have a lot to talk about. That had to be the year's winning understatement.

Once Kit was dispatched to get ready for bed, Savanah rounded on Beau. "Let's have it,'' she demanded without preliminaries.

"I was wondering when we'd get around to having this little discussion.''

"Don't you dare sit there and grin at me. I demand to know why you claim we're still married. We had an attorney take care of the annulment nearly six years ago.''

"So I thought. It seems your esteemed counselor was just a shade shady. That's what you get,'' he said with mock reproach, "for picking a lawyer from the Yellow Pages."

"But he was paid. What happened?"

"I guess he was pressed for time. No doubt he had to get out of town in a hurry with our money. He either forgot or simply neglected to file the papers."

Savanah dropped into a chair, her legs no longer capable of supporting her weight. "I don't believe it. It has to be a mistake."

"It isn't. Believe me, I had it checked out thoroughly before coming here. My lawyer assures me that you and I are still very much married. At least in the eyes of the law."

"But how did it come to light now, after all these years?"

Beau sat in a chair opposite her. "It was uncovered in a routine check. For a prenuptial agreement."

Savanah looked up at him with surprise. "A prenuptial agreement? You're getting married?"

"Well, I was. My fiancée had qualms about marrying a bigamist and the wedding was called off."

"But why? Didn't you explain it was just a legal snafu that could be easily corrected?"

"Can it?"

"What do you mean, can it? Of course it can."

"Maybe not. Too much time has elapsed for us to obtain an annulment now, so we'll have to initiate divorce proceedings. Then there's the question of community property."

And custody of a minor child, she thought with growing horror. Hiding her turmoil she said, "Then start initiating. I don't want anything from you except a piece of paper that says it's over between us for good."

"That might be a little premature. I think we should take our time and think about things this time. We parted in haste once, let's not do it again. Who knows, maybe we won't want to get divorced."

"Are you crazy? If we couldn't get along before, what makes you think we could now?"

"Like I said, people change."

"Like *I* said, not that much, they don't. Besides, we have no feelings for one another."

"We don't? Then why does my pulse go crazy when I look at you? When I remember how it used to be?" He leaned toward her and his hands spanned her waist.

"Don't let your famous bedside manner get the best of you." Savanah jumped up and went to the window where she found comfort in the familiar inky darkness. How many times had she stood so, wondering where Beau was, what he was doing? How often had she wondered if he was gazing at the same starry sky and thinking of her? Wondered whether the moonlight that bathed her tear-streaked face washed over him? "Those feelings will go away when you do. I don't want to repeat a foolish mistake. Last time it nearly ruined the lives of two people."

"Which two people were those, Savanah?" Beau asked softly.

"Don't do this, Beau. Just don't do it."

"Do what?"

"What you do best. You bewitched me into eloping with you. I didn't know what hit me. One minute

I was studying for finals and the next I was in your bed. I didn't act rationally, I was so drunk with…'' her voice trailed off. She couldn't finish the thought, much less the sentence.

But Beau could. ''Drunk with what, Savanah? Love?'' He came up behind her and wrapped his arms around her.

She stiffened at the familiar touch but allowed him to turn her around, regretting it when she realized how close his lips were to hers. ''Passion, Beau. And that's all it was. Temporary insanity aggravated by over-worked postadolescent hormones.''

''If I really believed that, we wouldn't want each other so much, and I wouldn't be here now,'' he whispered, his words fanning her lips with his warm, sweet breath.

She wrenched away but not before she felt herself responding to him in a very basic way. The knowledge that he still had a power over her was frightening. It was a fear she knew all too well. When she'd realized her impulsive marriage to Beau endangered the safe security of her uneventful life, she'd panicked and fled. She wanted to flee now, but she forced herself to remain calm. ''If I didn't believe it, I wouldn't allow you to be here.''

''You say it, but you don't mean it.'' Beau sat on the love seat and patted the space beside him. ''Now that we've gotten the obligatory pass and disparaging words out of the way, can we sit down and discuss this like two adults?''

Savanah eyed him and the narrow seat. ''I'd rather keep my distance, if you don't mind.''

"I always admired your honesty, Savanah. I'm glad to see you're still truthful about some things."

"What's that supposed to mean?"

"It means I know you feel the same pull I do. It means I have to wonder why you never told your family about us."

"I told them I'd been married, but I didn't want to distress them with the sordid details."

"Like my name?"

She ignored his pointed reference. "Besides, I felt it would be easier to just try and forget."

"And did you?" he asked softly.

"It wasn't easy." She might have succeeded if it hadn't been for one little thing—a six-pound, four-ounce little thing. Pippy and Jasmine had been troubled by her evasiveness regarding her baby's father, but they'd shown a great deal of courage and had given her their full support during her "time of trial."

They'd taken over shortly after Kit's birth, allowing her to pursue her career. She'd always known what she would be when she grew up. Her fascination with medicine had begun at age five when Doc had first allowed her to wear his stethoscope.

She'd practically grown up in the clinic and when she was old enough to be of real help, Doc had put her to work organizing the clutter in his office. When the time came he made sure she was accepted at Emory. The money she earned during summer vacations, and the financial aid he'd helped her obtain, paid for her education.

Doc had hoped she'd go on to medical school, but Savanah liked nursing and had promised to be the best nurse she could be. She owed him a lot. Not only had he encouraged and supported her in her career goals, but he'd never once asked any painful, personal questions. He'd never lost faith in her, and friendship such as his was priceless. Savanah turned her wandering attention back to Beau when he spoke again.

"I don't think we should be so hasty about this divorce thing. Maybe it's not too late for us. Don't we owe it to ourselves to give it another shot?" He wanted to ask about Kit's father but was reluctant to bring up a topic that was sure to put even more distance between them.

"Any debts between us were paid a long time ago. I think you should leave quietly, have your attorney draw up the necessary papers, and mail them for my signature. Go back to Boston. To your fiancée and your life and let me get on with mine."

"Is that what you're so upset about? My fiancée?" he asked quietly.

She wanted to say no, that she couldn't care less, but lying had never been easy. She said nothing.

Beau continued, "For your information, I have no fiancée and my life will take place anywhere I want it to. Right now, Harmony, Georgia is looking pretty damn good."

She felt his eyes on her, his heated gaze touching her in ways she didn't want to be touched. Already the memories of their brief life together were crowding out rational thoughts. "Just because our paths crossed once in the past doesn't mean there's any future for us. Do us both a favor, and go away before things get out of hand again," she insisted.

His response was postponed when a small voice called from the doorway. "I'm ready, Mommy, will you come and tuck me in?"

Eager to escape Beau's penetrating gaze, Savanah bolted from her chair. "Of course, baby."

"Good night, Dr. Beaulieu," Kit said formally, holding out his hand to be shaken.

"Good night, Kit." Beau took the tiny hand and fought down the impulse to pull the child into his arms for a big hug. He told himself again that the similarities of their upbringing made him feel a kinship toward the child. That explained the tightness in his chest and such uncharacteristic emotion.

Savanah watched the two, and her heart nearly broke at the light in Kit's eyes. How much brighter it would glow if he knew Beau was the father he'd never known. Was Kit's capacity for understanding sufficiently developed to handle such a revelation? Was her own?

She resented Beau's sudden appearance and the implications it might have. She'd struggled to rear Kit the best she knew how. Alone. She'd given birth alone. Alone, she'd walked the floor with him while he teethed, watched him lurch to his feet for his first tentative steps. In light of their relative stakes in Kit's past and future, she could hardly sit by and allow Beau to blithely assume a role in her son's life now. She might consider sharing him, but she couldn't bear the idea of losing her son, even to his father.

If Beau discovered her secret, he was sure to do one of two things: hate her or run for the nearest attorney to sue for custody.

A silence so profound that it drew attention to it-self hung heavily in the air, and Kit filled the breach. "Are you really going to stay for a while, Dr. Beau-lieu? I heard Granny Pip tell Auntie Jasmine that a young scalawag like you wouldn't last long in Harmony."

"Kit!" Savanah's embarrassment was acute.

"Never mind, Kit," Beau soothed. "I understand her reservations."

Reassured that he hadn't said anything wrong, Kit continued his story before Savanah could lead him away. "Auntie Jasmine said if you start doctoring here all the young women in this town would fall sick for sure. Said it don't seem proper, somehow."

"Kit!" Savanah reached for his hand, but Beau drew the child into his lap.

"Really? What did your Granny Pip say to that?"

"Well . . ." Kit stared at a spot on the ceiling, as if trying to remember, his small face puckered in concentration. "Oh, yeah, she said, *Jasmine, if it'll ease your mind, I'm sure Dr. Beau's interested in our Savanah and won't fall prey to them. Surely he can control any las...lassie...some kind of urges.*" He looked up for help.

"Lascivious?" Beau prompted with a grin.

Kit nodded triumphantly. "Yeah, them kind."

Clutching the doorframe in white-knuckled embarrassment, Savanah tapped her head against it in frustration. Unfortunately, Kit had total recall when it came to overheard conversations.

"What'd it all mean?"

"I think it means Granny Pip doesn't think too badly of me as a person or a doctor."

"That's good, 'cause I like you."

"I like you, too." Beau gave the child a squeeze, finding simple joy in the sweet, soapy clean smell of him. His flannel pajamas were soft from many washings, a comforting tactile sensation recalled from his own childhood.

"Come along, Kit," Savanah prompted. "It's way past bedtime. Tell Dr. Beaulieu good-night."

" 'Night, Dr. Beau."

"Good night, son."

Son? Savanah turned away quickly, taking her child, her guilt and her fear with her. When she had Kit tucked snugly into bed she dawdled, picking up toys, closing drawers, prolonging the moment when she would be alone with Beau again. In his presence she didn't feel like a capable woman of twenty-seven, who was a single mother committed to her career and responsible for two elderly women.

When she was with Beau she felt like the giddy young girl who'd once let her heart rule her head with disastrous results. She didn't want to go back downstairs and thought that if she lingered long enough, he'd get tired of waiting and leave, not only the house, but town. But deep down she knew he was too stubborn to give up that easily.

"Mommy?"

"Yes, Kit?" Savanah sat on the edge of his small bed.

"I like Dr. Beau," he proclaimed wistfully.

"Well, that's fine, sweetie. But you mustn't spend too much time with him." She steeled herself for the questions she knew would follow.

"Why not?"

"Because he's only here for a little while. He's a doctor and he won't have time for little boys."

"Aw, I ain't so little. I have a birthday coming up soon."

"That's right. How would you like to have a party?" She was planning a celebration for his fifth birthday but had refrained from discussing it too far in advance since his concept of time was still vague.

"Can we invite everyone we know?"

"How about just your closest friends?"

"Great! How many more days?"

"Fifteen and you are only allowed to ask that question once a day until then. Deal?"

"Deal." Kit wrapped his tiny arms around her neck and gave her a moist, noisy smack. "I love you, Mommy."

"I love you, too. Go to sleep and happy dreams." She kissed him again, her heart tightening with the joy of having been given such a wonderful gift. His unqualified love filled up her life and made the emptiness of the years seem unimportant.

She switched off the light, closed the door and leaned against it, fighting the urge to lock herself in her son's room. But that wouldn't lock Beau out of her thoughts or her heart.

Instead she went to her room and changed. She knew she had to go downstairs and resume their interrupted conversation. But she didn't want to spend any more time alone with Beau than was necessary. In fact, she didn't want to do anything that might make her change her stubbornly madeup mind about Gordon Beaulieu.

When they'd separated she'd thought she would die—but she hadn't. She'd survived and she had Kit to show for their brief time together. She'd picked up the pieces of her life, carving a niche for herself in Harmony where her roots went deep.

She'd been only sixteen when her widowed mother married and moved to California, but she'd elected to stay with Pippy and Jasmine. She'd sensed that while her mother had the fulfillment of new love, the old ladies had only each other. Besides, going to California meant taking a risk and she wasn't a risk taker. She preferred the known to the unknown and readily admitted she had no sense of adventure. She needed predictability to feel secure, security to be happy. Long ago she'd confronted the question of whether she was using Pippy and Jasmine as an excuse not to live life fully; she had dismissed it as nonsense. They needed her, and she needed to be needed.

Maybe it was a little boring and unexciting by some standards, but Savanah was content with her quiet life and had never objected to dull. Beau, on the other hand, had always believed the hype about only going around once in life and had seemed determined to do it in the most exciting way possible.

Maybe he had changed, but she couldn't accept that he'd changed enough to ever consider settling permanently in a place like Harmony. If he really was planning to stay a while, she'd find that out for himself

soon enough. Her problem was to make sure he didn't
also find out the truth about Kit in the process.

Fate had brought him back into her life and,
whether he knew it or not, they were bound together
by the strongest tie a man and a woman could share—
parenthood. She knew it wasn't fair to keep father and
son apart, but it was necessary and she would do it.
Kit's life must not be affected by Beau's sudden in-
trusion. Her determination made her feel mean and
selfish, traits she'd never known she possessed.

After she'd changed, Savanah found Beau on the
porch swing, looking more handsome in the moonlight than a man had a right to look. The night was
seductive, lying close like a warm second skin. The air
was rich with the scent of newmown grass damp with
dew. Cicadas nibbled the edges of the silence and a few
wary stars flirted overhead.

"It was such a nice night, I couldn't resist coming
out for a little porch swinging." He set the swing in
motion with his foot and grinned engagingly. "Join
me?"

She stood in uncertainty, her arms folded across her
chest, and he noticed she'd changed clothes. In the
uniform she'd looked all business, but in the pink
denim overalls and T-shirt she appeared a sexy, vul-
nerable waif. She was barefoot and he couldn't resist
teasing her. "You always were a heathen when it came
to shoes. A real country girl."

She rubbed the top of one foot with the sole of the
other. "And you always pestered me about my shoe-
shucking habit."

He grinned, recalling that the teasing usually climaxed with him tickling her small feet and nibbling her dainty toes. He could tell by the look on her face that she was remembering, too, and was suddenly overcome with the desire to do both, right now. "Come swing with me," he urged.

She arched a brow. "The last time I did that, I woke up with a ring on my finger." She disregarded the warnings her common sense frantically telegraphed and sat down beside him.

"This one?" He opened his hand and held it out for her to see. The plain gold band she'd worn so briefly caught the moonlight and reflected it back.

"You kept it for all these years?"

"I came home one day, and it was the only thing of yours left in our apartment. The next and the last time I saw you was in the attorney's office."

"I needed to put some distance between us." Truth to tell, she'd been afraid to see him alone. His sweet-talking was like a powerful drug, and when she was with him she felt invincible. She was able to think rationally only at a distance, so she'd stayed with a girlfriend until departing for Harmony. The only way she could have met with Beau was under those constrained circumstances.

His arm stretched out along the back of the swing and his fingers brushed her neck and drew her near. "I didn't want distance between us then, and I still don't."

She pulled away. "Maybe the law says we're married, but I made my choice when I left. As far as I'm concerned, that marriage never happened."

"What about this?" He took her hand to drop the ring in her palm, but she snatched it away.

"It no longer belongs to me, everything between us is over. Get used to the idea."

He leaned back and rested one sneakered foot on the opposite knee, recalling how difficult it had been at the time. "I tried. And I didn't care for it. You really dealt my ego and pride a deadly blow when you walked out on me without any explanation."

"I left a note."

"Oh, yes. The 'Dear Beau' letter. All you said was that you'd made a terrible mistake, that we were too different to ever be happy together. I believe you cited financial background, social status, family tree and irreconcilable value systems as contributing factors."

She frowned at his facetious tone. "You knew our marriage was a mistake from the very beginning."

"What gave you that idea? I was a loving, considerate and sensitive husband."

"You were loving...but...everyone knew..."

"Everyone? Everyone who? Why did you run away? If only you'd confided in me...talked to me."

"We never talked, that was the whole problem. What we did was—"

"Yeah, I remember. Beats talking all to hell, doesn't it?"

"You're doing it again," she warned. "Can't you be serious?"

"You want serious? Then I suggest you give me a long overdue explanation."

How could she explain? Savanah rose and leaned on the porch railing. Someone as self-assured as Gordon

Beaulieu regarded acceptance as his due, and he would never understand how much his world had overwhelmed her. She couldn't explain, because even now, after all this time, she didn't fully understand her feelings herself.

She sighed and made an attempt. "Remember that party we attended about a week after we were married? I can't recall the hostess, but her name was Muffy, or Cissy, or Bootsy or one of those names rich people give their children and poor people give their dogs."

"It was Buffy," he corrected.

"Oh, yes, Buffy. At the party, I had the dubious privilege of overhearing a very interesting conversation. Some of your friends were bemoaning the sad fact that you'd somehow gotten yourself stuck with a country bumpkin and were speculating the reasons thereof.

"I listened shamelessly, and it's true—eavesdroppers never hear good of themselves. Anyway, it came up that poor Christine Bayer, of the Boston Bayers, was devastated by our betrayal. It seems breaking your engagement to her brought on a depression so acute, only a trip to Europe could cure it."

"Wait just a minute. I wasn't engaged to Christine Bayer then."

"That's not the way I heard it."

"Why didn't you ask me? I could have set the record straight."

"Since you'd never even mentioned this longtime sweetheart, how could I trust you to be honest about it?"

"That's it? That's your measly explanation? You left me over a silly misunderstanding generated by a couple of airhead debutantes?" Beau's voice had escalated considerably. "I never mentioned her because there was nothing significant about our relationship to discuss."

"Will you please keep your voice down? Do you want the neighbors to hear you? Worse, do you want Kit to? He's got a tape-recorder memory as you already know. Besides, there was more."

"Pray tell me."

"Their boyfriends joined the conversation and one of them mentioned that he'd heard your mother was furious about you marrying a 'little hick nobody' and was going to cut you off. With no money from home, it would have been impossible for you to finish medical school and support a wife. They intimated that as far as they were concerned, you'd dug your own grave and had a glorious career at the car wash ahead of you."

"Dammit, Savanah. You're smarter than that! Did it ever occur to you to talk to me about what you'd heard?"

"Yes, it did," she said softly. "I laid awake nights watching you sleep and cursing myself for ruining your life. I tried to tell myself that what I'd heard was just jealous gossip. But when your mother showed up on our doorstep a week later, so underwhelmed to meet me, I knew it was all true."

"Is that why you suddenly invented a sick friend to visit? You were afraid of my mother?"

"Well, don't look so surprised. Your mother is a very scary lady." The intimidating Catherine Hampstead Beaulieu had quickly made Savanah feel inadequate and ill at ease.

"I'll concede that. But why didn't you come back?"

"I did. I heard your voices raised in something less than rejoicing when I climbed the stairs. Eavesdropper that I am, I wasn't too proud to listen outside the door and I heard the whole ugly scene. Your mother's predictions matched your friends', but she was hoping to *pay the little tramp off*. And if you didn't agree to an annulment, you'd never get another penny from her. If you didn't get your M.D. you wouldn't inherit the money your grandfather left you."

"You heard the prosecution, so why didn't you hear the defense?"

"At that point I left, went to a movie. I sat through it, twice, trying to decide what to do."

"So that's where you were. At some lousy movie making a decision you had no business making without a fair discussion." Beau's fist came down hard on the arm of the swing. "When you didn't come home I went looking for you. I was frantic. Isn't that ironic?"

"I'll bet your mother wasn't worried at all."

"You should have stuck around for act two. You might have gotten a kick out of hearing my undying declarations of love. But keep in mind that I was young and stupid then, and I believed the song about my love being all you really need."

She sighed. "I was afraid you'd say something dumb like that. And I didn't want to be put in the middle." Looking back she realized that it had been a no-win situation. If he'd chosen her, at the expense of his family and inheritance, there was the possibility he would have grown to resent her. Even in her blackest moments she hadn't really believed he would choose the money over her, but she had finally decided not to risk the pain of finding out for sure. She'd opted to take the choice away from him because she'd loved him so much.

"It really didn't seem all that dumb at the time, it was the way I felt. I told mother my becoming a doctor was important to me but not as important as you, and if she couldn't accept our marriage, then it was her loss, not mine. She finally realized she had no choice when I vowed I'd shine shoes to pay my way through school, and to hell with her precious money."

Savanah looked at him incredulously. "You could have told me these things that day at the lawyer's office."

"I was too young and impulsive—and you can add 'too proud' to the list. It hurt that I was willing to give up everything and you were ready to throw it all away. You wouldn't talk to me on the telephone, your friend always said you were out. I finally got your message."

When she didn't say anything, he crossed to the railing and pulled her to him fiercely. "I don't know why I came here, Savanah, I only know it was something I had to do. But I sensed I'd never be happy, and it would never be over and done with until we got everything out in the open. There's still something between us that I can't label. Call it love, or lust, or unfinished business; it's there and always will be until we finish it properly. What we had was special, maybe I just wanted the chance to have it again."

She melted into the warmth of his embrace and before she knew it, his mouth was on hers, searing it with a rekindled passion that surpassed what they'd shared before. She felt a sense of homecoming, of being where she belonged at long last. The feelings she'd kept in check for so long threatened to consume her.

Then she remembered that nothing had truly changed. They were still worlds apart. A society doctor could hardly have a nurse for his wife, and she wouldn't give up the career that meant so much to her.

Despite his professional curiosity about small-town medicine, he'd never forego a lucrative Boston practice, and she could never leave her home. Not for a life that was as foreign and unfamiliar as that of an extraterrestrial. And what about Pippy and Jasmine? It would break their hearts if she took Kit away.

Kit was another good reason why she mustn't listen to Beau's sweet words. Since divorce was inevitable, she couldn't bear the thought of her son being hurt, of being caught in a painful custody battle. She struggled out of his arms. "Don't, Beau. Let me go."

"What's wrong now?" He feared he already knew the answer. There was someone else—or at least the memory of someone else. She hadn't found Kit in the cabbage patch. "Were you thinking of Kit's father? Where is he, anyway?"

It wasn't as if she hadn't expected him to ask, but because he'd asked now. "What difference does that make?"

He grasped her shoulders and held them gently, but firmly. "It matters," he said slowly. "Is he dead?"

"He might as well be." A heavy sadness dulled her words.

"Did you love him?"

"Very much."

"And you can't give yourself to me because of him?"

"I don't know," she mumbled. When he found out the truth, he was bound to hate her. What then? "It just wouldn't work. We've proven that. If our marriage was so tenuous and so lacking in trust that overheard conversations and pride could come between us, we'd be crazy to try it again."

"We were kids then, and we acted like kids. But we're older now and hopefully wiser. I'm not as idealistic as I used to be, and you're no longer a nervous bride, but I think we should find out what this thing is we still share."

"No, Beau. Believe me, it wouldn't work."

"Not if we don't try."

"Don't you see? I can't afford to explore any leftover feelings between us." Their passion was fiery, and Savanah didn't dare risk being burned again. If she let him back into her life, even for a few stolen moments together, too many people would be hurt when he left. And he would leave; he'd only be happy in a plush urban office surrounded by the accoutrements his position commanded.

"You can't deny what we're feeling."

"The only thing between us is physical attraction, a chemistry. I'll admit it's powerful, but it's not enough to base a relationship on. You'd better go now. I can't stop you from staying at Doc's. As they say, it's a free country. But don't expect to see me again. Our marriage died over five years ago. All we have left to do is sign the death certificate."

She went into the house, leaving Beau alone to consider the finality of what she'd said. He hadn't been able to accept it in the past and still couldn't, wouldn't accept that it was over between them now. He'd felt her response, and it was every bit as strong as his own. The old fire was there; it just needed to be fanned to flame.

He wanted her and intended to have her again. Possession was nine-tenths of the law and by God, she was still his wife. Their problem was they'd never had that all-important courtship. They'd married in the proverbial fever, eschewing the traditional trappings of social intercourse for the other kind. Now he wouldn't demand, he'd woo.

He walked across the street to Doc's house, already formulating a plan. His wife didn't know it, but a battle would soon be waged beneath the peach trees and magnolia blossoms of Harmony.

He considered himself well-armed for the upcoming campaign. He had a tenacity of purpose and an abundance of Yankee ingenuity, to say nothing of Yankee charm. And he could be relentless when he wanted something. If necessary, his seduction strategy would make Sherman's march through Georgia look like a Sunday outing.

He grinned as he let himself into the house. It promised to be a hell of a tussle and he wouldn't guarantee his tactics would be honorable in the tradition of the Old South. But then, wasn't everything fair in love and war?

Chapter Three

From the looks of the little group, they were coming from the church up the street, the one whose bell had begun pealing at an unholy hour. Since he was awake anyway, Beau had taken one of Doc's magazines out to the front porch to enjoy the clean air and country sunshine.

He watched Savanah gracefully maneuver the cracked sidewalk in her high-heeled shoes and noticed again what a great pair of legs she had. Her apple-green suit and white ruffled blouse weren't tailored to excite anyone's prurient interests, but nonetheless, they did a fair job on his own.

The Magnolia Brigade, as he'd dubbed Pippy and Jasmine, was a vision in pastel dresses and tiny veiled hats. Kit, who skipped along between them, looked like a pint-size banker in a suit, vest and tiny bow tie.

Beau tucked the magazine behind a porch pillar and stepped out to the sidewalk to greet them. "Morning, ladies. Kit. Beautiful day, isn't it?"

"I believe it's afternoon," Savanah pointed out.

He checked the sun's position. "Why, so it is."

"Dr. Beau, if you're still in town you must join us for services next Sunday," Jasmine implored. "Reverend Dunwoody is downright inspiring."

"I'm sure he is."

Savanah looked at him pointedly. "Yes, please do. The good reverend is always looking for lost lambs to save." But who'd save the lambs from the wolf? Word of the arrival of a new and exotic male had gotten about quickly, no doubt due to the reliable Friday-night-bingo-tongue-waggers' grapevine. Judging by the gossipmongered before, during and after the sermon this morning, the bored young ladies of Harmony were already discussing potential sacrifices.

Misty Rose Clayborne had promptly volunteered solely on the basis of Aunt Jasmine's description of the newcomer. Others, less desperate, would hold out until they saw him in the flesh. Savanah expected a steady stream of slow-moving traffic to tour past Doc's house today hoping for a glimpse of the man in question.

"Did Doc get away on his trip all right?" Pippy inquired.

"He left first thing this morning," Beau answered. "Said he knew there was a five-pound bass with his name on it in that lake, and he intended to claim it."

"Milt always did love to fish," recalled Jasmine. "Why, I remember..."

"Never mind the trip down memory lane, Jasmine," scolded Pippy. "How long are you planning to stay, Doctor?"

"At least until Doc returns. I have a few weeks before I have to get back to Boston." He watched Savanah to see what effect his announcement would have on her. Considering the way they last parted, it hadn't surprised him that she'd stayed behind closed doors the day before, not even allowing Kit out to play. But she couldn't hide forever. Like it or not, when she reported for work tomorrow, he'd be there.

"What do you think of the clinic?" asked Pippy.

"Doc has a nice little operation, but it's a far cry from what I'm used to. I think I'm going to enjoy the less frenetic pace." Before he left Doc had given Beau a quick tour of the antiquated six-bed clinic that was currently empty of patients.

He'd explained that most people chose to go to the hospital in Atlanta, sixty miles away, but he maintained the beds for the old-timers who didn't trust modern medicine and big cities, and for emergency cases.

Beau was fascinated by Doc. The old man had never married, saying most women didn't understand a mistress like medicine. After a stint in the medical corps during World War II, he'd returned to his hometown to practice and had been there ever since, ministering to the townspeople as well as to those on outlying farms. Many depended on him because they had no insurance, and he allowed them to pay as much as they could afford.

Most physicians Beau knew spent more time with their accountants than with their patients. At the busy hospital where he'd completed his surgical residency, patients were sometimes reduced to numbers on medical charts by necessity. The absence of personalized care had often disturbed him, and he was already thinking of ways to incorporate some of Doc's philosophy into his own work.

"Small town practice can be mighty satisfying," Doc had pitched. "The hours are long, you rarely have a day off, and you live poor as a church mouse. But the rewards are many. If you go down to the square on a Saturday morning, half the people you meet were delivered by me. I've seen a lot of souls come into this world, and I've had to watch some of them depart from it. But if I had it all to do over again, I wouldn't change a thing."

Recalling those words, Beau wondered if he'd be able to say the same in forty-five years. He wouldn't if he listened to his mother and kept living his life to suit her instead of himself. He wouldn't if he'd married Christine because everyone expected him to. At this point, he wanted to give marriage to Savanah another try.

She wasn't exactly willing, and she needed a little more time to get used to the idea. He wouldn't rush her, but he was sure that if she gave him half a chance, they could rediscover the rapture they'd once known. That sense of fulfillment had been missing from his life far too long. He rather hoped it had been missing from hers as well.

"It's been nice chatting with you, Beau." Savanah took Kit's hand and turned away. She couldn't believe he was actually going to stay. Not after she'd made it clear there was no future for them. But then, Beau always had been stubborn.

What Gordon Beaulieu wanted, Gordon Beaulieu got. But not this time. Not if she had anything to say about it. The best thing to do, she decided, was to be as cool as possible and not give him any encouragement. When offered an inch, he habitually took a mile.

"Wait, Savanah." His voice was soft and undemanding, but suggested he was accustomed to having women do his bidding. "Won't you all be my guests for lunch? I don't know my way around Harmony yet, but perhaps you could suggest a suitable restaurant?"

Kit, heretofore observing the children-should-be-see-and-not-heard injunction, suddenly came to life and blurted, "Can we go to the Catfish Corral? Can we, please?"

The name conjured up visions of underwater roundups, complete with seagoing cowboys and waterproof branding irons. "Is that your favorite place?" Beau asked.

"I'll say! They have all the fish you can eat and the best hush puppies in the county. All the kids get to dive into Capt'n Cecil's treasure chest and last time I got a compass."

"It sounds...charming." Beau turned to the ladies. "What about it? May I repay you for the fine

supper of Friday night by treating you to all the catfish you can eat?''.

"Don't forget the hush puppies," Kit reminded.

"Why, that would be lovely, wouldn't it, Pip?"
Jasmine cooed.

"It would indeed. There's nothing more enjoyable
than going out to eat after church when you're all
dressed up. We would be happy to accept your generous invitation, Dr. Beau."

"Yippee!" Kit squealed in delight.

Beau had reservations about the place, but if it
could elicit that kind of response from Kit, it couldn't
be all bad.

Savanah felt trapped. Of all the things she didn't
want to do, sharing another meal with Beau topped the
list. "Pippy, you and Jasmine will mind Kit, won't
you? I'm afraid I've developed an awful headache and
can't go."

A headache? That sounded lame, she berated herself. She was a nurse, and that was the best she could
do? Why hadn't she come up with something less ordinary? Like leprosy?

"We don't mind, dear, but are you sure you won't
come along?" Pippy's tone revealed her suspicions
about the instantaneous nature of the attack.

"Dr. Beau, don't you have some remedy for poor
Savanah?" Jasmine entreated. "Some newfangled
drug that will knock that nasty old headache right
out?"

Beau grinned and ignoring the don't-you-dare look
Savanah shot him, turned and bounded up the steps.

"As a matter-of-fact, I do. Now don't go away, I'll be right back."

He was. He took Savanah's hand and dropped two small tablets into her palm. "Take these with water, and they should do the trick in no time at all."

She glanced at the wonder drug. Aspirin. He'd seen through her ruse and was calling her bluff. He closed her fist over the medication, and for a moment she considered throwing it into his grinning face. Not the aspirin. Her fist.

She didn't like the way his touch made her feel, so she snatched her hand from his. "Thank you," she said ungraciously.

"Just doing my job."

"Temporary job."

"In for a penny, in for a pound."

"Don't remind me," Savanah muttered.

Beau had to call lunch a success. Savanah was civil, only kicking him under the table twice. Pippy and Jasmine had introduced him to as many of their friends as they could scare up, and Kit had fished a pirate's eye patch out of Capt'n Cecil's treasure chest. It wasn't exactly the romantic interlude he'd have preferred, but it was a beginning. Start small and think big. That was his motto.

Pippy and Jasmine volunteered to put Kit down for his nap before retiring to their rooms. Beau explained that Doc had been in such a hurry to leave that he'd neglected to show him the patient files and asked if Savanah would accompany him to the clinic and show him where everything was. He was pleasantly surprised when she consented.

She followed him to the wing that housed the clinic and went inside. He closed the door and leaned against it.

She turned to him with an okay-buster-let's-get-this-over-with glare. "You didn't get me over here to explain the filing system."

"What was your first clue?"

"For starters, your clumsy attempts to engage me in a game of footsie at the Catfish Corral."

"Clumsy? Sensitive, modern women do not call a man's romantic overtures 'clumsy.' I'm surprised at you."

She sighed in exasperation. Romance had never been one of his shortcomings. "Then maybe I should have called them unwelcome. Is that easier for your tender ego to accept?"

He pretended to look disappointed. "A bit."

"Was there something you didn't understand Friday night?" she asked him. "I thought I made my feelings perfectly clear."

"On the contrary, I don't think you're letting your feelings get involved at all," he said silkily, moving closer.

"Keep your distance, or I'm going home right now," she warned. "I want to get something straight. Are you going to give me a nice quiet divorce, or do I have to pitch a fit? Because if I do, I might as well get started."

"I want two weeks."

"To do what?" she asked.

"To find out if there's any hope for us. All I ask is that you give us a chance. Then if you still insist on the divorce, you can have your lawyer take care of it."

"I'd rather the good people of Harmony didn't get involved in this. Especially Pippy and Jasmine. Can't we just keep it between ourselves?"

Beau recognized a wonderful opportunity for blackmail, which under most circumstances he'd be loathe to employ. But desperate situations required desperate actions and successful people were those who seized every opportunity. "I'll be happy to keep your little secret for you."

"Why do I sense there's more to that sentence, and it begins with the word 'if'?"

"You always were perceptive, Savanah. I'll keep our marriage a secret, *if* you'll give me a chance to get you out of my system."

How romantic. "If it's purging you need, as a nurse I can suggest a few over-the-counter remedies."

He laughed. That was something else he'd always liked about her. She was very quick. "I'm not making any untoward suggestions."

"Could have fooled me."

"You don't have to do anything you don't want to do, and I'll take care of the details. All you have to do is keep an open, receptive mind."

"But that's..."

"I know," he said, shaking his head in mock disgust. "Blackmail. Such an ugly word, and full of unsavory connotations. Try to think of it as a case of 'I'll scratch your back if you'll scratch mine.' Or any other appropriate part of the anatomy."

The thought of that much physical contact made her uncomfortable. "I prefer to think of it as blackmail."

"Suit yourself. Is it a deal?"

"What choice do I have?"

"None that I can see."

"Then I guess it's a deal."

He took both her hands in his, pressed a tender kiss into each of her palms and closed her fists over them.

Savanah tried but was unable to make any objections when he slipped his arms around her waist. Rational thought disappeared when his gaze captured and held hers.

All she could see was her reflection in his eyes. All she could feel was his heart beating against her own. All she wanted in the world was for him to kiss her.

Obliging soul that he was, he did. His right hand slid down her back in a gentle massaging motion and molded her abdomen against the proof of his desire.

Savanah's hands went around his neck and she forgot all about protesting. Thoughts of everything but his nearness vanished like smoke in the wind.

He searched her face for the slightest sign of rejection and finding none, pulled her closer. His lips brushed hers gently, almost reverently, before parting them and deepening the kiss.

Her long-repressed emotions sizzled and her body clamored for his touch. Involuntarily, Savanah swayed against him, joy, like a silver spring, welling up inside her. The velvet warmth of his kiss brought back memories of nights when such kisses were only the prelude to so much more.

Drowning in the dreamy intimacy they shared, he smoothed both hands over Savanah's bottom, finding remembered delight in its shape. His hands followed a course of their own, charting, searching her body, knowing instinctively what they sought.

Savanah touched his chest, and her fingertips feathered over his upper arms, relearning the muscles, the bones, the tendons. She relived the wild range of feelings he'd helped her discover years before, feelings that had been put on hold for so long.

This loss of control was how it had all started. Nothing had ever remained simple with Beau, and Kit had resulted from just such a seemingly innocent encounter.

The thought of Kit was enough to return her to some semblance of sanity, and she pushed away from him. "Stop, Beau," she said when he tried to take her into his arms once more.

He took a deep breath and leaned against the wall, staring at his hands as though not quite believing where they'd been, the liberties they'd taken. Even if she were his wife, this was not how he'd planned to win her over. Quickly, before they got him into more trouble, he stuffed both hands into his pockets.

"I didn't mean for that to happen," he said truthfully.

"Didn't you?"

"No." He added with a sheepish grin, "Not yet, anyway. it's just that every time I get near you, I forget."

"Forget what?"

"I forget all about noble intentions, that it's supposed to be over between us. That our marriage exists only on paper." He stepped over to the counter and fingered a stethoscope.

"I don't think that's something we should forget. If you're serious about spending the next two weeks here, we'll simply have to establish some kind of ground rules."

"Such as?"

"For starters, I'd like to be able to do my job without being chased around the examining table. I think we should adopt a hands-off policy." Her tone was businesslike, but her emotions were still charged.

"But—"

She halted his interruption. "I'll agree to keep an open mind, if you'll agree not to use unfair diversionary tactics."

"Like that kiss?"

"That's a good example. The only thing between us is a strong sexual attraction, and it's unfair of you to use it when you say you want to find out if there's more to us than that. I refuse to work with you if you plan on kissing me every time we're alone. Do I make myself clear?"

More damn rules! He'd always rebelled against rules. "Perfectly. It'll be difficult, but I hereby promise not to take unfair advantage of our mutual attraction." Before he made that vow, he'd been careful to cross the fingers of the hand still in his pocket. It was a ridiculous promise anyway, how could he be expected to keep it?

After agreeing to that uneasy truce they toured the clinic, and Savanah pointed out the things she felt he should know before he saw his first patients. Then she left.

Beau watched her, noting the way she stopped at the curb and looked both ways before stepping into the street. What a cautious woman.

"What a woman," he amended as he turned and sauntered toward the kitchen to make himself at home, as Doc had exhorted him to do. Taking a soft drink from the refrigerator, he went out to the backyard to look around.

He admired the bud-laden branches of the flowering shrubs that marched along the property line, and the neat flower borders where green things were already shooting up through carefully applied mulch. A huge clump of daffodils nodded in the sparse shade of a big oak. Doc obviously enjoyed gardening, his expertise was apparent in the lushness of the lawn and the manicured perfection of each flower pot.

Settling down under a gnarled magnolia, Beau contemplated his situation. Was it destiny or blind luck that had saved him from that fate worse than death—marriage to Christine Bayer?

It was funny the way things had worked out. He'd like nothing better than to find that shyster lawyer who was responsible for him still being married to Savanah. Find him and thank him.

If he hadn't been so crooked, Beau wouldn't be sitting in the shade of a Georgia magnolia, his lips still tingling with the memory of Savanah's kiss. He'd be perched on the edge of a Louis XIV couch in the Bayer sitting room, a Wedgwood cup of Darjeeling tea in his hand, going over a list of wedding guests with Christine and her dragon of a mother. Maybe his own dragon of a mother would be there as well, giving freely of her unwanted advice.

Yes, he decided, he owed that crook a lifelong debt of gratitude. If it hadn't been for him, he might never have found Savanah again, might never have met little Kit, with whom he felt an inexplicable bond forging.

Beau massaged his forehead with the cold can and reclined in the fragrant new grass. He closed his eyes and saw two sweet faces stamped firmly beneath his lids.

Savanah tossed and turned on the pillow, the nap she'd been so determined to take was a dismal failure. There was no way she was ever going to sleep. Not that she'd rested much the night before, nor was the likely to as long as Beau was on the scene. Her plans to keep him out of her life were doomed if his touch could still wreak such havoc with her self-control.

Last night she'd had dreams of an undeniably erotic nature, dreams of intimate nights spent in their tiny apartment, dreams fraught with longing and desire. She'd woke calling his name softly in the darkness, her body damp and straining toward something no longer there. She'd been reluctant to close her eyes again for fear the dreams would return and leave her even more frustrated than she was already.

Since sleep was neither possible nor desirable now, she got up and straightened the covers out of habit.

She'd never been one for naps, so why begin now? Looking around, she wondered if it was time to update the room. She could get a new bedspread to replace the girlish, lacy white one that had covered the bed since her high-school days. Then she'd have to change the rose-sprigged wallpaper and the ruffled pink priscillas with billowing sheers. While she was at it, she might as well get new furniture.

She had neither the time nor the energy for such an undertaking, and besides, she liked the old-fashioned room. It suited her. Beau had called her an old-fashioned girl often enough.

Beau. It was all his fault. Seeing him again had made her feel restless and dissatisfied with things as they were. No doubt about it, that man was going to prove a disruptive influence in her quiet, tidy life. He'd always been the impetuous, throw-caution-to-the-wind type. Rocking the boat and overturning apple carts were his favorite activities, and she had a sneaking suspicion that he'd taken a special interest in her particular apple cart. But she wasn't about to let the upheaval begin in her own bedroom.

She should have known better than to think of bedrooms and Beau in the same context. The idea sparked a warm tingly feeling, and she hurried to the open window to cool off. It was late afternoon and the neighborhood was quiet.

She positioned herself so that anyone watching from across the street wouldn't see her. Mindful to stay behind the sheer curtains, she trained her gaze in the direction of her thoughts.

And not a moment too soon. She spotted Kit jumping off Doc's porch steps and racing around the house to disappear into the backyard.

Savanah flounced out of the house and marched across the street when she learned Aunt Jasmine had given Kit permission to "call on Dr. Beau."

"It's the neighborly thin' tah do," Savanah mocked under her breath as she knocked on the door. "What in the world had come ovah you?" she mimicked, glad that Aunt Jasmine didn't know the half of it. She couldn't let Kit spend any time alone with Beau, it was too dangerous. Beau was naturally curious and not above asking a little boy personal questions. Given Kit's penchant for repeating things, Beau was sure to obtain information she didn't want him to have.

When there was no answer at the door, she slipped around the corner of the house and peered through the bushes. She drew in a sharp breath when she caught a secret glimpse of the only two men in her life—together.

Kit was seated as close as possible to Beau on the soft new grass, mimicking his pose. Beau selected a blade and put it between his teeth. Savanah's eyes misted when Kit did likewise. They looked so right together, so natural, that it nearly broke her heart. How could the man not realize the child was his? She blinked back the tears and made herself more comfortable, listening unashamedly as their voices wafted over to her. She didn't want to disturb them. Not just yet.

Kit looked up into Beau's face and smiled. "You ever do much tree climbing, Dr. Beau?"

He grinned and winked at the boy. "Not lately. I'm as rusty at that as I am at banister sliding. But I was about your age when I learned how."

"Did your daddy learn you?"

Beau patted his thin shoulder, marveling at the sturdy muscular strength of the small frame. "No. My father lived far away. My cousin taught me," he said, automatically correcting Kit's grammar.

"I don't have no cousins. I wish I had one to show me stuff." His voice became wistful. "What I really wish I had is a daddy."

Poor kid. Beau discarded his blade of grass and smiled when Kit did the same. "You don't have a daddy," he echoed, encouraging the child to talk about it if he wanted to.

"I don't think so." Kit looked thoughtful, then with all the conviction he could muster, added, "Nope. I'm pretty sure I don't. I been thinkin' about it a lot, though. All my friends got daddies somewhere, some of 'em even has two. But I don't have one nowhere. It ain't fair."

"No, it isn't." It was none of Beau's business, and he knew he should change the subject, but he liked the boy. Dammit, every kid had the right to know his father, no matter who or where he was. "Maybe you should discuss this with your mother." Beau vowed not to get involved after that suggestion. In light of the little Savanah had told him, he didn't think she'd take kindly to he and Kit having a private conversation on the subject of fathers.

"Aw, I'd better not. I wouldn't want her to cry or nothin'." Kit squinted up at Beau as if waiting for a response.

He didn't have one.

The terrible picture of Savanah in tears over some other guy did strange things to Beau and he felt sorry for the child and for her. She'd been cryptic on the subject, but the only logical explanation was that Kit's father was dead—no man in his right mind would have left them.

"Aren't there any pictures of your daddy?" There went that vow not to pry.

"Nope."

"Does your mommy cry a lot? About your daddy?" He was nosing in where fools were too wise to tread, but he couldn't help himself. He had to know.

"Nope."

"What makes you think she'd cry if you asked about him?"

"One time I asked Auntie Jasmine, and she started in sniffin' and her eyes got all teary and red. Then she started huggin' me and stuff and tellin' me she was sorry. I don't know what she did, but I didn't tell nobody," Kit said proudly. "A guy don't rat on his friends."

"You'd be a good friend to have, Kit. Want to be mine?"

"Sure. I wish you was my cousin, though. Or my daddy."

Beau blinked, nearly choking with surprise. "Why?"

Kit flashed him a toothy grin. "Then you could learn me stuff."

Beau pursed his lips thoughtfully. "Friends can teach each other lots of things. I'll be happy to teach you anything I can, and you can show me a few things, too. How does that sound?"

"Okay, I guess." Kit frowned. "But I don't know very much yet, I'm just a lil' kid."

"You're not so little."

"I'm almost this many," Kit waved one hand, displaying all five digits.

Beau smiled. Kit was small for his age. "You're almost five, huh? When's your birthday?"

"In thirteen more days. Will you come to my party?"

"I'd be honored. I wouldn't want to miss my best buddy's big day."

Kit beamed as if he'd just had a wonderful idea. "I know what! If you teach me how to climb a tree, I'll teach you how to catch lightning bugs when they come out."

Beau knew he wouldn't be around when the insects made their first appearance, but there was no point telling the boy that. "That sounds like a good deal to me. That's what buddies are for, isn't it?"

Beau was rewarded with another big grin. "Yeah."

He couldn't resist touching the winsome, charming little boy so he gave him a mock punch on the arm. "If I'm going to teach you how to climb a tree, we'd better get started before you have to go in for supper." Beau got up and rubbed his hands together.

Kit rubbed his hands too, before squinting up at him. "I'm ready."

Beau surveyed the yard, looking for a likely conquest. "Doc sure has a lot of nice plants. I never seem to have much luck with them. Guess I just have a brown thumb."

"Really? Let me see."

He chuckled. "It isn't really brown, that's just what people say when they have trouble getting things to grow. I usually kill every plant I come in contact with." Fortunately, he was a much better surgeon than gardener.

"Maybe Mommy can help you. She's real good at that stuff. I guess her thumb's not brown like yours."

"Hers is probably green," Beau said absently.

"Nope. Just plain like mine." Kit shrugged. "Which tree are we gonna climb?" He pointed to the tall, sturdy oak by the gate, and a look of misgiving crossed his face as he leaned back, one hand on his hip, to see the top. "That there one is sure high."

Savanah saw Kit pointing and scrunched down so she couldn't be caught spying and crying. The overheard conversation had affected her more deeply than she'd have thought possible, and she wanted to get herself under control before confronting them. On second thought, she'd just wait until after the tree-climbing session that seemed to be in the offing. She wasn't too confident about Kit's athletic ability and none too sure about Beau's teaching qualifications, but she knew she could trust him with her son's safety.

Beau saw the look of doubt on Kit's face. "You'd better start with something a little more your size.

That oak looks like a level-two tree if you ask me." He sauntered in the direction of a young elm with small, low-hanging limbs.

Savanah breathed a sigh of relief, granting Beau this private time with his son. She realized she wanted Kit to have these few moments alone with his father. Neither of them knew, might never know of their relationship, but their time together was sacred, nonetheless. It was something beautiful, something to be honored.

"Aren't you comin' up, too?" Kit asked as he trustingly placed his foot in the stirrup Beau made with his hands.

"I'll be the ground control and watch you from down here. If you get into trouble, I'll be able to help. Okay?"

"Okay. But I won't go too far," he promised.

"Good." Beau smiled at the child's attempts to reassure the man. "Just remember to hang on with both hands and feet. Always hold on with one hand, while the other reaches for the next branch. Got that?"

"Got it." Kit scrambled shakily up to the first limb.

"Move one foot to the fork of the next branch . . . yeah, that's the way. Now reach with your hand and pull yourself up," Beau instructed.

"I can't, Dr. Beau," Kit huffed. "My shoestring's caught on something."

"Hang on, son, I'll help you." Without thinking the process through, Beau swung himself onto the lowest branch with the grace of Spiderman. He could see where the sneaker lace was snagged on a twig, immobilizing Kit. Standing on the limb and inching his way along, he smiled reassuringly at the boy on the branch above and painstakingly removed the sneaker from his foot.

Kit flung himself at Beau, and he caught him to his chest. They wobbled precariously for a moment before Beau regained his balance. "Okay, one piggy-back ride going down."

Kit giggled.

Once on the ground Beau knelt in front of the child. "Tree climbing can be fun, but it's serious business, isn't it?"

Kit nodded solemnly, eyes big and round.

"It's also something you shouldn't do on your own for a while, until you really get the hang of it. Okay?"

"Okay." Kit's eyes shone up at him.

"I'll make a deal with you, anytime you want to go up, you just let me know and we'll do it together. Deal?"

Kit grinned and shook the hand offered him. "You got a deal."

Beau ruffled his hair. "Let's go see if we can find a cool drink, I worked up a powerful thirst. How about you?"

The boy nodded. "I'm so thirsty, I'm spittin' cotton."

Savanah, still hidden, watched as the two walked side by side into the house. She knew her heretofore peaceful existence was a thing of the past. Standing, she put her hands to the small of her back, stretching from her crouched position behind the bush.

"Hello," sang Maybelle and Lavern, bingo buddies of Pippy's and Jasmine's, as they waved tentatively from the sidewalk.

"Oh, hi, ladies. I'll bet you're wondering what I was doing down there, huh?" Savanah stalled as heat flooded her face.

Maybelle and Lavern exchanged there-always-was-something-strange-about-her-looks.

"Doc went fishing, and I promised to check out his—"

"Hi, Mom, waiting for me? We saw you from the window, and Dr. Beau said you were probably—" Kit jumped off the porch and ran to greet her.

"I said you were probably checking the bushes for root rot, like Doc asked," he interrupted, coming to the rescue. He'd seen the whole thing and decided they should bail her out of this sticky mess. What he didn't understand was why she was sneaking around out here.

"Yes, yes, as a matter of fact that's exactly what I was doing. Not a rotten root in sight, thank goodness."

The ladies rounded the corner, but Savanah hung back. "Kit, why don't you run home and get cleaned up for supper. I need to discuss some patients with Dr. Beau. If I'm not home in time to eat, tell Pippy and Auntie Jasmine not to wait. I'll eat something later. Okay?"

"Sure." He shrugged, waved cheerfully and skipped off and called back over his shoulder, "See ya later, Dr. Beau."

"See ya later, squirt," Beau called with a wave. As soon as Kit was out of earshot he turned to her. "Poor kid looked like his fun was all over."

Savanah groaned inwardly. Everybody's fun would be over as soon as she lowered the paternity boom.

Chapter Four

"Are you trying to earn a badge in junior sleuthing?" Beau gave Savanah an appraising look. Her snug jeans and knotted-at-the-waist blue cotton shirt were more to his liking than that bulletproof Sunday-go-to-meeting outfit. Maybe Kit thought the fun was over, but what did he know? He was only four.

"No." She watched as Kit unlatched the gate and headed for home, his step made a bit lopsided by the missing shoe. "We have to talk. Privately."

"It's about time. But I'd still like to know what you were trying to prove by skulking around in the flower beds." He motioned for her to precede him through the kitchen door. "Alone at last," he sighed.

"Calm down, Dr. Heartbreak, this is important."

"What did you call me?"

She hadn't meant to let the old tag slip out. "I can't believe you weren't aware of what all the nursing students called you."

"Did they?" He hadn't known about the nickname, but he supposed it was apt enough. His reputation with the ladies, not entirely deserved, was such that his friends had been amazed he'd actually *married* a girl, who to their way of thinking could just as easily have been another conquest. They hadn't understood that she was special. "Even you?"

"Especially me. Try not to let it go to your head." She gestured at a kitchen chair and busied herself pouring glasses of iced tea from the pitcher in the refrigerator. "Stop fooling around and sit down. I have something to tell you."

"After you."

She'd been full of resolve earlier, but seated across the table from him, it was hard to remember what she knew she had to say. It was impossible to forget he was the only man she'd ever loved. The man who'd unknowingly fathered her child. The man who hadn't tried hard enough to prevent her from leaving him. The man who'd returned her letters unopened and unread.

"Come on, Nurse Goodbody. Get it over with. The suspense is killing me."

"What did you call *me*?"

"Don't tell me you didn't know that's what all the interns called you."

"You're making that up," she accused, smothering a self-satisfied grin.

"Nope, and it still fits, I see." He leaned back in his chair. "I thought you wanted to tell me something."

Over the years she'd nearly convinced herself Beau was nothing but an irresponsible, if adorable, rake who was totally wrong for her. A rich, spoiled young man who usually got what he wanted, only to lose interest when the novelty was gone. She'd never quite understood why he'd wanted so earnestly to marry her, unless it was because of the challenge she'd presented.

He was as adorable as ever, but maturity had tempered the irresponsibility. She wished he was snobbish and superficial and overbearing. That way she could dislike him with some degree of sincerity.

"Kit's birthday is coming up soon," she said meaningfully, hoping she wouldn't be forced to blurt out the whole story.

"I know. He invited me to his party. Do you mind if I attend?"

"I suppose not. He's taken quite a liking to you."

"He's a great kid."

"Thanks," she murmured, wondering why he hadn't figured out the significance of the birthday, which was precisely eight and a half months from the date of their alleged annulment. It didn't take a genius to put two and two together. But then, math had never been Beau's strongest subject.

"Good-looking little guy. I haven't been around many kids, but I like him. A lot."

Savanah nodded. Good-looking because his face is just a smaller version of the one you shave every morning, she thought ruefully. And you like him—gee, isn't that swell?

"I feel sorry for him, though."

She bristled. "Save your pity. He doesn't need that or anything else from you. We do quite well by Kit."

"Don't get all pushed out of shape, but I know how it feels to be a little boy in a house full of strict women."

"You haven't suffered from the experience, so what's your point?"

"No point. I just feel obligated to suggest that you loosen up a little. Let him get dirty, let him run instead of walk, let him learn a little independence."

"And what school of childrearing did you attend? Forget whatever feelings of obligation you may have. Kit is my business. How he's raised has nothing to do with you, and I'd appreciate it if you'd keep your opinions to yourself from now on." Savanah knew she was overreacting, but he had a lot of nerve.

It was just like Beau to successfully tap into her own doubts and uncertainties. What he said made sense, and it stung that he was right. The boy needed a father to teach him the little things she couldn't, but considering that Beau's only contribution toward Kit thus far was biological, he had no right to point out her failings as a parent.

Beau noticed that her eyes flashed in anger and . . . was it pain? Everything he'd heard about the female fighting for her cub was true. "I was only trying to help. I'm no authority on children, but I *was* a little boy once. I didn't have a full-time father either,

but at least I knew who he was. You owe it to Kit to at
least tell him about his father.''

"Oh, I do, do I? Do you think it's easy being a single parent?'' she snapped. ''Don't you know how
much I worry about him? About how his situation will
affect his development?''

He patted her hand and said gently, ''I'm sure you
do. You're a good mother.'' Something had been
nagging at Beau's mind since his earlier conversation
with Kit, and it was slowly forming a thought. If Kit
was soon to be five, then he would have been con-
ceived... His mind juggled the dates. Kit? Wasn't that
a nickname for...

"Savanah,'' he demanded, ''what is Kit's full
name?''

So, he'd finally figured it out, she thought. It had
taken him long enough. ''Christopher Jefferson
Winslow.''

"Christopher?''

"After his father, Gordon Christopher Beaulieu,''
she replied defiantly. She hadn't meant to tell him like
this, but he always had possessed the ability to make
her forget her good intentions.

He blanched with realization and slumped in his
chair. Now it all made sense. He understood why he'd
felt so close to the child, why there'd been something
familiar about him. Kit was his own flesh and blood.
His son. Why hadn't he seen it sooner?

Savanah watched Beau's face pale under his tan. It
hadn't been easy, but she was relieved to have the truth
known at last. The stress of trying to keep the relationship a secret was simply too much to bear. This

long overdue bit of air clearing was sure to change things.

Whether the change was for the better or the worse, remained to be seen. It would make the matter of obtaining a divorce a bit trickier, and she'd be forced to come clean with Pippy and Jasmine. It definitely complicated things, however, the burden of secrecy was just taken off her.

She took a deep breath and sighed. "You don't look too happy for a man who's just learned he's a father."

Beau stared at her for several long moments, then crossing to the sink, filled his empty tea glass with water. He gulped it down and wished he knew where Doc kept the whiskey. A man shouldn't have to absorb news like this on water alone. He'd heard Savanah's words, but they were slow to fully register in his benumbed mind. Not only was he married, he had a child. It was a lot for a previously unencumbered bachelor to take in.

"My God. At least you had nine months to get used to the idea of being a parent. I've had less than a minute. You started out with a tiny infant, but I'm presented with a forty-pound boy. Give me another moment, please."

"All you've been presented with is a few facts."

He was a father. He had a son. Despite his shock, he was filled with pride and an inexplicable sense of completeness. "Why didn't you tell me Kit belonged to me?"

Savanah counted to ten to slow her anger, slid out of her chair and paced across the room and back again. She'd anticipated this moment with both trepidation and longing. The reckoning had finally come and Beau was handling it exactly as she'd expected—by thinking of himself first. "Let's get something straight before we proceed. Kit is mine. Your only role has been strictly genetic."

Beau's anger mounted, and he fought for control. "You had no right to keep it from me, Savanah. To keep *him* from me."

She recognized the fury in his eyes, and his reaction touched off a spark of temper in herself. "Didn't I? As far as I knew, our annulment was legal. That meant our marriage never took place. That's the way you and your mother wanted it. You're the one with no rights."

"Maybe none you acknowledge, but what about legal rights? Moral rights? My God, he's my son, he belongs to me. You should have told me."

"I tried." Savanah's tone of voice had reached the same pitch as his, and she made an effort to lower it. "I tried."

"Oh really?" he asked incredulously. "I think I would have remembered something like that."

"I did try. When I found out I was pregnant, I wrote you a letter. You never answered it."

"*A* letter. As in one? One whole letter? What an effort that must have been. Pity I never received it."

"Give me some credit, will you? I wrote more than one. Not to ask for help but to let you know. I felt I owed you that much." She went to the window and stared out at nothing.

Beau's mind raced. There had been no letters, he was sure of that. He'd been so devastated after the annulment that he'd returned to Boston for the summer. His mother had gone to great lengths to help him "get over this messy little business" as she'd called his marriage. She'd arranged parties, tennis at the club and sailing outings. She'd hoped the social whirl would take his mind off Savanah and rekindle his interest in Christine.

When the time came to begin his internship, she'd pulled a few strings and arranged it so he could work in a local, but prestigious, hospital. He hadn't protested because there was nothing left for him in Georgia. "Where did you send those letters?" he asked with dawning suspicion.

"Where else? To your home in Boston. You told me at the attorney's office you were going back for the summer. The first one was never acknowledged, but I assumed that you'd received it. The others were all unopened and marked 'return to sender.' It didn't take long for me to realize you weren't interested in our child or in me."

An emptiness swelled inside him at the thought of what they'd both suffered. Especially Savanah. Pregnant and alone, she'd believed he no longer cared for her, that he hadn't even bothered to open her letters. Still, it hurt and infuriated him that she could have so little faith in him.

Most of his anger, however, was for his mother. He couldn't believe she'd been cruel enough to keep news of his child from him. He never thought she was that ruthless. "I didn't see those letters, Savanah. Mother must have intercepted them. As much as I hate to admit it, it sounds like something she'd do."

Savanah had to agree. Mrs. Beaulieu hadn't approved of her in the first place and had been the one to insist on an annulment rather than a divorce. She'd gone along because at that point it hadn't really mattered, the marriage was over. The means to the end weren't important.

Beau grasped Savanah's shoulders. "Did you hear me? I didn't see the letters. I never would've let you have that baby alone, and damn you for thinking I could. For weeks I thought of nothing but you and what happened. I went over and over the scenario in my mind, trying to understand what had gone wrong. For the preservation of my sanity, I finally had to convince myself that you didn't love me. I had to make myself believe you were right, that our marriage was a mistake.

"Then I threw myself into my work at the hospital in an effort to forget." His tone became wistful. "But it's always haunted me, and I've never gotten over it, or you." His next words were bitter. "Condemn me for being a spoiled, selfish young fool, but don't ever think I didn't care."

"Maybe you did once. But obviously you got over it."

"You never made an effort to contact me after that day in the lawyer's office, or at least that's what I thought. What was I supposed to do? Pine forever?"

"No. You were supposed to do exactly what you did. Start all over, fall in love and get engaged."

"Love!" Beau laughed wryly. "I'd married for love once and made a mess of it. I wasn't about to let that happen again. I simply allowed myself to get washed along in the tide of mother's and Christine's plans."

"Christine?" she asked. "You were going to marry Christine Bayer?"

"Christine happened to be between husbands, and I was feeling the pressure to settle down. Dr. Bayer, her father, offered me a partnership in his practice, and it seemed like the thing to do. I know it sounds callous, but—"

"It sounds heartless and materialistic."

"And safe."

"You must have loved her."

"No," he said emphatically. "I wouldn't call what Christine and I had *love*. It was more along the lines of trying to fulfill our families' expectations."

"I'm sure she's patiently waiting for you to come back all signed, sealed and delivered."

"Christine isn't known for her sense of humor. She got pretty nasty when I told her I was still legally married to you."

"That would be a hard thing for a bride-to-be to accept."

"Then her hard-nosed practical side won out, and she decided she could handle it. She tried to talk me into allowing her father's attorneys to take care of it so our wedding could go on as planned."

"Why didn't you? It sounds like the simplest solution to me."

"I don't know." He raked his hand through his curly hair. "I just didn't want some impartial stranger to knock on your door and break the news to you or your family. I know how protective you are when it comes to Pippy and Jasmine. I guess I wanted to soften the blow. At least, that's what I thought.''

"Well, now I know. You've told me. Go home and let your mother and Christine take care of this mess and the rest of your life."

"Give me some credit. If I'd wanted to marry Christine, I never would have come here and nothing would have changed my wedding plans. It took a while, but when I finally realized what a big mistake we were making, I called off the engagement. Forever wasn't in our future, and I wasn't willing to tie myself to her until she got ready to move on again."

"Commitment's a real toughie, isn't it?"

"When it's to the wrong woman. I never really loved her. I told myself I did, but there was nothing real or lasting between us."

The relief Savanah wanted to feel wouldn't materialize. Knowing him as she did, she couldn't believe he'd been about to enter into a loveless marriage. He'd married her in a fever of passion, why couldn't it have been that way with Christine? How could she trust his feelings? How could he trust his own? "What about our divorce? It'll be complicated somewhat by Kit, but..."

"Divorce? You can't be serious." Beau was trying to remain calm. "One thing at a time. I've just learned I'm a father. Let me get over that shock first."

"That news doesn't change a thing."

"How can you say that?" he asked incredulously. "My whole life has just been altered. I have a child. I have a responsibility."

"I, I, I, me, me, me! Listen to yourself, Beau. Your feelings aren't the only ones at stake here. I won't stay married to a man who doesn't love me, just because he fathered my child."

"Look who's talking! You won't this and you won't that! You're no longer the only one who has a say in this matter."

"What are you trying to say?"

"I'm saying, I think staying married is something *we* should think about and discuss." Their marriage had assumed its rightful place in his list of priorities. Before, just getting her back into bed had been a goal worth pursuing, now it seemed somehow dishonorable when it involved the mother of his child. "Besides it wasn't that bad, if memory serves me correctly. We had something once, maybe we could again."

"That all happened a long time ago. We're not those same young kids, we're different people now. We have to forget the past and get on with our lives."

"Forget? That's easy for you to say. You've had Kit all to yourself for nearly five years. Do you think I can go home and forget I have a son? Damn it, Savanah, you're a hard woman."

"This conversation frightens me." She turned to leave, but he grabbed her arm.

"What scares the hell out of me is, how do we tell Kit?"

A cold knot formed in her stomach. "I wish we didn't have to tell him at all. But more than that, I wish you wouldn't threaten me with it."

"For God's sake, woman." He paced around the table. "I have a son who doesn't even know I'm his father and a wife who wants a divorce. What am I supposed to do?"

"Don't look to me for answers. I don't even know what I'm supposed to do. Do you expect me to inform all and sundry that you're Kit's long-lost father? Make a public announcement in the town square? Is that it?"

"No one else needs to know if you're so damned worried about what all your dyed-in-the-wool Southern friends will think of you being married to a 'damnyankee.' You're blowing things all out of proportion, just the way you've always done, the way you did when you left me."

"Really? Do you suggest I tell Kit that his new friend, Dr. Beau, is also his father, but he mustn't tell anyone? Shall I explain that he was a by-product of a giant mistake?"

"I'm not suggesting any such thing, Savanah. Hell, I don't have any suggestions. All I know is that Kit and I have the right to know each other."

"So he can learn to love you and lose you?" The way she had. "Because he will lose you when you go back to your life in Boston. The fact that you're his father doesn't change that."

Beau looked at her blankly, certain he must have missed something. "I disagree. I think it's changed everything."

"Not really. I have my life, and you have yours. You'll go your way, I'll go mine. What could be simpler?"

"What makes you assume I'm going back to Boston now?"

As long as she thought he'd be leaving, she could distance herself from him. But if he stayed—even for a while—she couldn't face that. She jerked from his hold and ran for the door, intent on escape.

Beau caught her as she flung it open. He grabbed her shoulders and drew her into his arms. "Be warned. I plan to see that we at least try to stay together. As a family."

"A family?" She should have seen that coming, but she wasn't prepared for the force of will behind the words. He couldn't be serious. "I think the shock of instant fatherhood has caused temporary insanity. We've already tried marriage, remember? It didn't work then. And it won't work now. I can't leave Georgia, and you'd never be happy here."

"Do you think I can just walk away, Savanah? If you do, you're underestimating me. I won't let you end the marriage until we give ourselves a chance, until we find out if there's any hope for us." He added in a somber tone, "Even if there isn't, now that I know Kit is my son, I plan to be his father."

It was difficult to think straight when he held her so closely, but she reminded herself it was really Kit who was the object of his interest. How noble of him to take her as part of the package deal! "I didn't expect you to come back six years ago out of a misguided sense of duty, and I don't expect you to stay now."

"But you've forgotten a couple of little details. We're married and I'm here. I have just as much right to Kit as you do."

"How dare you waltz into our lives at this late date and say something like that! The only name on Kit's birth certificate is mine, and as far as I'm concerned, he's *my* son. I won't let you take him away from me.''

''I have a very good attorney now, but I have no intention of taking him away from you. I know what it's like to grow up with divorced parents, and I don't want my son to go through that unnecessarily.''

''So you're willing to stay married to me to spare Kit the hardship of a broken home? How big of you.'' Seeing the tempered determination stamped on Beau's handsome features made her even more sarcastic. ''I'm touched that you're so honorable. Your mother would be proud of you.''

''We'll leave Mother out of this for the time being, I'll deal with her later.'' His hands moved absently down her back, and she felt so right in his arms that he surprised himself by admitting, ''I don't know what I expected to find when I came here. I thought time might have dulled the intense feelings I've always had for you. I'm a little surprised and pleased to discover the attraction is just as strong as ever. I halfway expected you to be a stranger to me, but it didn't quite turn out that way.''

''No, you found out you have a child, and that's a heady sensation. But we both know guilt and duty and body chemistry are no basis for a marriage.''

''I resent you speaking for me. I don't think guilt or duty have a damn thing to do with the way we feel.''

''Now you're speaking for me. Who says I feel anything for you?''

''I do, and I can prove it.'' His lips sought and found hers in a crushing kiss. He pulled her to him until her breasts flattened against his chest, and she could feel his heart pounding with all the fury of her own. His tongue quested after hers, and she felt consumed by him.

She wanted to push him away, to escape the mind-drugging intensity of his kiss. She couldn't think properly when he held her, his touch brought back too much. But she knew that was exactly what he hoped to do, make her forget everything but how much she wanted him. She had to get away, before he succeeded.

"Dammit Beau, stop. You promised not to do this," she said in halfhearted protest. Squirming, she tried to wriggle from his arms. "Don't."

"Don't? Do you want me to stop or not?" he teased. "Why fight it? You know how good it can be between us. Doesn't this prove something?" He dipped his head for another kiss, but she turned hers away.

"Yes, it does. It proves I was right all along. It proves we share a strong physical attraction, but that's still not grounds for marriage.

"It can't hurt," he muttered with a devilish grin.

"Beau, will you please be serious?"

"All right." He released her, and she moved away from him. "You want serious, how's this? I want Kit to know I'm his father."

"Not yet. You can't just spring something like that on a child. It could cause irreparable emotional harm." Savanah leaned against the doorframe, her chest rising and falling with each gasp of air. "He must be prepared."

Beau leaned over her, his outstretched arms pressed against the doorjamb to hold his body away from hers. "I don't think he'll find the news so devastating. I'm not such a bad guy, and he already likes me."

"My point exactly. He does like you. Think what will happen to him when you leave. 'Hello, I'm your father. Goodbye.' Try to imagine how hurt and rejected he'll feel."

"You don't know that's how it will be." Should he tell her he'd been asked to join the staff of a hospital in Atlanta? That he'd come to see for himself what the position had to offer? No, that could wait. She'd feel even more threatened if he told her the distance she was trying to put between them was mostly in her heart. He'd take it one step at a time.

"It doesn't matter what your plans are. You won't be staying here, so the whole question is academic. You simply can't tell anyone you're Kit's father, especially Pippy and Jasmine. They'd fall over in a dead swoon, and I'd never hear the end of it. Not only that, but they'd lock you in the cellar to keep you here."

"With you? That has interesting possibilities."

"Stop trying to distract me. I'll concede Kit has a right to know about you, but I don't want him to hear it from gossips. I want to break the news to him gently and avoid as much trauma as possible."

Based on their conversation in the yard, Beau didn't think Kit would have any problem handling the fact he had a father, but if that was the way she wanted to play it, he'd go along for a while. He needed time to get his own life in order. "All right. But I want to know when you'll tell him."

"When the time is right," she evaded.

"And when will that be?" he persisted.

"When I decide it is. When we've worked out the details. Don't pressure me on this, Beau. I think I know what's best for Kit. I know him better than you do."

That much was true, a situation he planned to correct. "We'll do it your way. But I won't wait forever. If you insist on going ahead with a divorce, be warned that I'll take steps to make sure I don't lose Kit. I've missed enough of his life as it is. I'll go to court if I have to."

Savanah's eyes snapped with blue fire and a colorful flush crept over her face. "What's that supposed to mean?" she snapped. She didn't like being threatened, and that was a threat if she'd ever heard one. How dare he use her child as a weapon against her!

"It means that whether or not you and I are able to work things out, I still want Kit."

"You want! You always get what you want, don't you, Dr. Gordon Christopher Beaulieu the Third? What about what I want?" She didn't give him time to respond before continuing angrily. "Did I want to go through my pregnancy frightened and alone? Did I want to give birth, after an eighteen-hour labor, with only Doc, Pippy and Jasmine to share my joy? I didn't *want* you to come blundering into our lives just when I'd found some peace." Tears threatened, but she wiped them away with her hand. "Did you ever once stop to consider what I wanted?"

"That works both ways. Okay, you were hurt and alone, and for that I am truly sorry. But what about me? Don't you think I've been hurt, too? I've missed out on a lot in my son's life." He tried to touch her, but she pulled back.

"Just leave me alone. It's getting late, and everyone will be wondering what in the world we're doing over here. I'm going home because I don't want to talk to you right now. I'm too mad."

She ducked beneath his arm and ran out the door.

"Savanah, wait. We have to resolve this."

"Not tonight," she said firmly, her tone bitter with old resentments and pain. "Give me time to cool off and think about things. I'm not in the mood for negotiating, and it wouldn't take much for me to choke you right now."

She stomped across the street without glancing in both directions, and Beau knew the extent of her turmoil. So, she was upset, was she? Dammit, so was he. How dare she run away when there were important issues to be discussed and settled. That was just like her.

When it came to dealing with problems, he was the full-out, head-on type. It made him furious that she'd taken her marbles and gone home.

He clamped down on the bitter accusation. He remembered that she was an exasperating woman. But maybe that was part of the attraction. Maybe what they'd shared wasn't love, still, there was something to be said for passion. It wasn't reserved for love alone. It was logical that the physical ardor they felt would carry over into other aspects of their relationship.

He had feelings and rights too, whether she realized it or not. He'd have to show her more tenderness, convince her there was a chance for a workable arrangement. He'd make her understand if it was the last thing he did. He wasn't one who gave up easily.

Beau could be persuasive when the situation warranted, but he hadn't been too successful at charming Savanah so far. However, he had the satisfaction of knowing he had her outnumbered. Kit was sure to be on his side, and he felt confident that if he played his cards right, he could win the support of Pippy and Jasmine as well. When they learned the truth they'd be more than amenable to aiding his cause.

He'd read the fear, hurt and anger in Savanah's eyes, and those were not the emotions he wanted to see there. He made another vow that before the next two weeks were out, her eyes would reflect desire for him instead.

What was that old saying? You could catch more flies with honey than with vinegar. He'd been a fool to lose his temper and put her on the defensive. That crack about going to court had been nothing short of stupid. He'd have to be more careful, their emotions were too fragile right now.

She'd goaded him into using vinegar this time, but he had an ample supply of honey as well. He'd be the very model of sweetness. He'd be so sweet the whole damned town would get cavities.

Or his name wasn't Dr. Heartbreak.

Chapter Five

Beau fixed himself a sandwich, but he wasn't hungry. He tried to watch television, but he wasn't interested. He stared at a book, but he couldn't concentrate on the words. He couldn't stop thinking about Savanah and their child.

She said she needed time to cool off, to think things through. Maybe that's how she handled a problem, but it wasn't his style. He preferred to deal with things in a direct manner. Waiting had never been his forte.

He tossed the book aside and paced the room, recalling their conversation. She'd twisted things around until he'd become the villain of the piece, and he resented that. It wasn't his fault that she'd walked out on him. That decision had been her own. He wasn't completely responsible for her being alone when she had Kit. God, he'd have given ten years of his life to have witnessed such a miracle.

He went outside and sat on the porch, feeling lonelier than he'd ever felt before. He had a family, yet he didn't *have* one at all. He stared at the house across the street, imagining the homey scenes being enacted within. The upstairs was dark, except for the soft glow of what he presumed was a night-light in Kit's room, indicating that his son had already gone to bed. Beau wondered if Savanah had read to the child before turning out the main light, then wondered which stories were the boy's favorites. It hurt that his son would soon be five, and he had yet to read him a story.

There was so much he'd missed out on, so many irretrievable milestones and events, that it didn't seem fair for him to be excluded now. For nearly five years Savanah had been tucking their son into bed, kissing him good night, loving him. For nearly five years she'd known the joy and anguish of parenthood.

Beau had been a father for less than two hours, yet he'd already experienced the incredible elation, felt the terrible pain.

Pippy and Jasmine had raised their questioning eyes when Savanah returned from the clinic in a dither. To their credit they seemed to sense she was in no mood for conversation, and Kit had provided a necessary distraction by requiring help with his bath.

After he was settled for the night, Savanah returned to the parlor and pretended to read a magazine while Pippy and Jasmine played a game of gin rummy. Jasmine was in her element because a former flame, a professional gambler, had taught her how to cheat. Pippy was the only one in Harmony who would play cards with her.

Jasmine drew a card and made a great show of re-arranging the ones in her hand until they suited her. Then spreading them like a proud peacock would his tail feathers, she slapped them down on the table with a self-satisfied flourish. "Gin. Again."

Pippy scraped all the cards into a pile with a frown. "I quit," she snapped. "Why I let myself get suckered in by a sharper like you is beyond me."

"What about my winnings, Pip?" Jasmine inquired archly.

"So sue me," Pippy taunted.

Savanah sighed. She hoped they weren't warming up for another feud. In 1965 they'd gotten into an argument over whether Truman or Eisenhower had done the most for the country, and they hadn't spoken again until 1967. True, that particular cold war had been great fun. She'd been a little girl at the time and served as go-between and relayer of messages. Both sides had attempted to buy her undying loyalty with all manner of forbidden treats.

If they drew the battle lines now, however, it would just be one more thing for her to worry about, and she scarcely had time to do justice to her current assortment of annoyances.

"Are you going to welch on our little bet?" Jasmine quipped, as shocked as she might have been had Pippy announced she was joining a club whose members gardened in the nude.

'I believe the term is welsh," Pippy corrected. "If you're going to bad-mouth a body, at least do it in proper English."

"Well, I never." Jasmine's hanky fluttered furiously in front of her indignant face.

"I know you never. If you had, like as not you wouldn't be such an old prune."

"Phillipa Jane Potter! I declare, sometimes you can be so nasty," Jasmine snapped. "For your information, the word is welch. W-e-l-c-h."

"Welch is the grape juice people, you old fool."

"Welch means to swindle by going back on your word. Only the lowest forms of humanity do it. You wouldn't dare."

"You're a hardheaded old broad. It's w-e-l-s-h," Pippy spelled distinctly. "And you think I wouldn't do it? Just hide and watch, Sister, just hide and watch."

"Please," Savanah interceded. "Must you argue over something so silly?"

"It isn't silly when someone owes you . . ." Jasmine checked the tally, " . . . three dollars and forty-five cents. And welches on it."

"Welsh!" Pippy repeated stubbornly, folding her arms across her chest as if that settled the matter.

Jasmine's eyes narrowed. "Welch."

Savanah's nerves could take no more. "Why don't you just look it up in the dictionary?" she snapped before stalking to the window to stare out at the dark street. She focused on the single downstairs light in Doc's house.

"Well, Miss Smarty-Pants, why don't you look it up for us?" Jasmine huffed, shocked by her niece's uncharacteristic display of temper.

Savanah paced to the bookshelf and took down the Webster's. "I refuse to get involved." She handed the book to Jasmine, kissing her soft, lined cheek. "You look it up. Then you two please play nice." Giving her grandmother an equally gentle kiss, she said, "I'm sorry I barked at you. I love you both very much, I don't know what came over me."

"Well, I do," Pippy disagreed. "I may be old, but not so old I don't recognize the symptoms. You haven't been yourself since that young doctor arrived. Love sometimes makes a body do strange things."

"Now just never you mind, Savanah. Auntie Jasmine knows just how you feel. I've been in love before," she commiserated.

"Back when Hector was a pup," scoffed Pippy under her breath.

"Love!" Savanah nearly screeched, forgetting her usual regard for the ladies' delicate sensibilities. "Whatever gave you the silly notion that I'm in love. That's ridiculous."

Pippy and Jasmine exchanged knowing smiles and nods, as if Savanah's adamant denial had only proven their point.

"Don't do that!" she exclaimed. "You don't know what you're talking about."

Jasmine tittered behind her hanky. Pippy's smile broadened, and she gave Savanah an exaggerated wink. "It's all right, dear. We'd have to be blind not

to know that you and Dr. Beau were more than col-
lege chums. Anybody with eyes can see he'd like to
rekindle the romance. You can tell us everything."

"There's nothing to tell," Savanah protested.
Nothing? Who would have suspected the old dears of
being so perceptive? Did they really have any idea of
her former relationship with Beau or was it simply the
wishful thinking of born matchmakers?

"Of course there isn't," Jasmine soothed.

"Not a thing," Pippy agreed.

Savanah would have argued, but a loud rap on the
front door cut short further discussion.

"Beau! What are you doing here?"

"I'm here to talk." He leaned forward, both hands
braced against the doorframe.

"I told you I'd talk to you later," she whispered.

"I know. But the more I thought about it, the less I
liked that idea. Why should you be calling all the
shots? You should know me well enough to realize I'm
not the calm-down-first, talk-later type. I want to talk
now. I'll think about calming down tomorrow, or the
day after that."

"Keep your voice down, Kit's in bed, and Pippy and
Jasmine are in the parlor."

"Good. Maybe they need to hear what I have to
say."

"You wouldn't dare. You promised to wait until I
was ready to tell them," Savanah hissed.

"Tell us what, dear?" Pippy asked from the parlor
doorway.

"Nothing." Savanah spoke too quickly.

"Oh," the ladies said in unison. "*That* kind of nothing."

Mistaking Beau's anger for passion of a different kind, Pippy prompted Jasmine with a bit of judiciously applied body English to the ribs. "Perhaps we should retire and allow the youngsters some privacy."

"Excellent suggestion, Sister." Their earlier argument forgotten, they mounted the stairs arm in arm, their gray heads bobbing conspiratorially.

Beau clutched Savanah's hand and pulled her into the parlor, closing the double doors after them with a thud. "I've decided you have no right to be angry with me," he announced.

"Is that so? I was under the impression that American citizens have the unalienable right to be angry with whomever they choose." Savanah plopped down on the settee, her arms folded across her chest.

He sent her a withering glance. "I don't want to play games with you, I just want to get something settled between us."

"I thought we agreed to discuss it when we were both in a more tolerant mood."

"There was no agreement on my part. I was flattened by the impact of the guilt you hit me with. But after you left I got to thinking, and I realized that I wasn't the only one at fault. We both made mistakes, and we've both paid for it. I think I've paid a dearer price than you, but that's beside the point."

"What?" Savanah hadn't meant to raise her voice.

"Forget I said that. We've both suffered. Period. But it's time for the suffering to stop. I didn't want to come over here tonight, I wanted to give you the time you asked for. But the longer I sat in that house, alone, the more I needed to see you. To discuss this." And to touch you, he added silently, making the move to do just that.

Savanah leapt up and dashed behind the settee. "I'd rather you didn't."

"Which of us don't you trust? Me or yourself?" he asked.

She spoke with a calmness she didn't feel, ignoring his question. "Okay, I'll acknowledge we've both suffered. Go on."

Beau sensed it would be bad strategy to push her, though he wanted very much to take her into his arms and kiss her protests away. "Since we'll be working together at the clinic tomorrow, I didn't think we should leave matters so unsettled between us. I wouldn't be able to concentrate fully on the patients." He watched her face soften, knowing he'd appealed to her sense of duty.

"And...?"

"And the bottom line is, I want access to Kit. I want to spend time with him. I want time to get to know him. Time for him to get to know me."

Savanah didn't speak, but considered his request thoughtfully. "What else?" she asked at length.

"That's it. For the time being. I won't tell him or anyone else that I'm his father, but I won't be denied any longer."

"Shouldn't you substantiate that with a threat regarding possible litigation?" she snapped. She hadn't meant to sound so hard, but she'd had time to think as well and she was afraid. "I won't allow you to use

Kit against me, and I won't be subjected to emotional blackmail. I know the powerful Beaulieus have more resources than I, but if push comes to shove, I'll make you sorry you ever started a custody fight.''

"A custody fight? Lord, you can jump to conclusions like a champion steeplechaser jumps hurdles. Just as you did nearly six years ago when—'' He broke off in midsentence when a distinct thud sounded in the hallway. A moment later the door opened and Pippy's head poked around it.

"Dr. Beau, come quickly,'' she cried. "It's Jasmine.''

Beau reached the fallen woman first. He knelt beside her, searching for a pulse while Savanah peered anxiously over his shoulder and Pippy hovered nearby.

"What happened to her?'' Savanah asked. "Did she faint, or slip or what, Pip?''

The old woman's brow creased, and she wrung her hands in agitation. "I don't rightly know. It was so suddenlike. I just don't know.''

Beau gathered the frail Jasmine into his arms and carried her into the parlor, laying her gently on the settee. "Her pulse is a little fast, but it's strong.'' He directed Pippy to loosen her sister's clothing and ordered Savanah to retrieve his medical bag from Doc's house.

She hesitated, reluctant to leave her beloved greataunt for a moment. She stared at the sofa where Jasmine lay so deathly pale and still. "Oh, Beau...'' Her voice cracked, and she crumpled into his outstretched arms for solace. "Please don't let anything happen to her. I love her so much.''

Beau held her tightly. "I know." He gave her a last lingering squeeze. "Go on, now. Hurry."

She glanced over his shoulder for another quick glimpse before leaving his comforting arms. Then, much to her surprise and relief, she saw that not only were her aunt's eyes open, they were bright and alert. Savanah opened her mouth to speak, but Jasmine shook her head and winked saucily.

Beau's gaze followed Savanah's to his patient, and he knelt beside her once again. He was pleased that she'd regained consciousness and seemed coherent. "Are you having any pain?" he asked gently.

"Well," Jasmine said in a voice weakened by a coughing spasm. "Not really. I declare, I must have swooned. I'm sure I'll be all right in a little bit." Her voice trailed away as though speaking were too great an effort, and she collapsed on the cushions, throwing her arm over her eyes.

Pippy, who'd been clutching a needlepoint pillow to her chest, turned away from the little group and pressed her face into it. Her shoulders shook.

No doubt with hysterical laughter, Savanah thought. What were they up to with all this playacting? Incurable snoops, they must have sneaked back downstairs to eavesdrop and overheard her arguing with Beau. Unable to resist a chance to meddle in her life, they'd taken matters into their own conniving little, blue-veined hands.

After confirming as well as he could that Jasmine was in no immediate danger, Beau went for his bag himself, saying he would do a more thorough examination when he returned. Little old ladies simply did not collapse without reason, he thought as he dashed out the front door.

"Aunt Jasmine, you old faker," Savanah whispered the moment Beau was out of earshot. "How could you? You scared me to death."

"Well," Jasmine returned defensively. "I'm sorry about that, but somebody had to do something. Pippy wasn't any help, she was just a-standing there with her mouth hanging open."

"It isn't every day a body learns who her great-grandson's daddy is, you know," Pippy said. "Lordy, Jasmine, you were wonderful." She patted her sister's thin shoulder and cackled delightedly. "You should be on the stage, or maybe TV."

Jasmine ducked her head modestly, then looked up. "Was I really convincing, Pip?"

Pippy hooted. "I could scarcely keep a straight face when you made me wait to call them in until you'd arranged your skirts all properlike." She admonished, "I didn't know you had it in you, Sister, how did you ever think of such a thing?"

"I don't know what came over me. Inspiration, I reckon. What about the way I fluttered my eyes and coughed? Wasn't that a nice touch?"

"I'll swan, if I hadn't known better, I'd have called the undertaker, right then and there," Pippy complimented.

"Hush, both of you," Savanah demanded. "This has gone far enough. I can't believe you two would stoop to such antics."

"We couldn't bear to hear you and Beau fighting. It just seemed like the thing to do at the time," Jasmine explained.

"Your acting was very convincing, Aunt Jasmine," Savanah told her. "Are you willing to go to the hospital to sustain this little farce?"

"I'm fine. I don't need to go to the hospital."

Pippy frowned. "But she will if she has to. We can't let Beau think badly of us, now that he's going to be a member of the family."

"He isn't!" This wasn't at all the way Savanah had planned to break the news of her marriage to Beau.

"If Beau is Kit's father, then you must remarry." Jasmine was adamant. "At once."

"I don't have to remarry him."

"Of course you do. It's only proper." Pippy was arbiter of all things proper.

"But you don't understand—"

"It's you who don't understand, young lady," Jasmine cut in. "Decent men marry the mother of their children, and I think Beau's a decent man. Family honor is at stake."

Savanah was losing control of the situation. The family honor was just as intact as it had ever been, but she wasn't about to tell these budding Sarah Bernhardts that. They would make her life unbearable with all their questions if they knew she was still legally married to Beau. To change the subject, she said, "He'll be back in a minute, and I think this time would be better spent planning a way out of this mess you've created for yourselves."

"Don't let them take me away to a hospital," Jasmine wailed.

"For two cents, I'd have both of you carted away by the men in the white coats for staging this little drama."

"We were only trying to help. Just remember that harsh words between lovers are hard forgotten," Pippy implored.

Tears filled Jasmine's faded blue eyes. "I'm sure you'll both thank me someday. It's better that you won't have to forgive each other later. I didn't mean any harm."

Both lined and wrinkled faces looked so pathetic Savanah wanted to take the old ladies into her arms and comfort them. "I'll help you out of this, but you have to promise not to interfere ever again."

"Why, I'll swear on a stack of Bibles a mile high," Jasmine vowed, secretly crossing the fingers of one hand beneath her full-skirted dress.

"That goes double for me," Pippy said solemnly, crossing the fingers of both hands beneath her apron.

When Beau opened the front door he heard laughter floating out of the parlor. Shamelessly, he listened and learned the truth about Jasmine's alleged fainting spell. He found the situation amusing, but judging from her reaction, Savanah lacked his finely tuned sense of humor. She was threatening to have the old dears committed to a home for the criminally nosey.

Suddenly aware of his presence on the stairs, he looked up and saw Kit, dressed in his pajamas and rubbing his eyes. Knowing there was no emergency, he climbed the stairs to his son. "What's wrong, Kit? Couldn't you sleep?"

"I heard people yelling. Is somethin' wrong?"

"No. Everything is fine. Come on, I'll put you back to bed."

Kit went willingly and hopped under the covers. "Did something bad happen to Auntie Jasmine?"

"She's perfectly all right, don't worry about a thing. She and Pippy were practicing their acting." He'd give the ladies a chance to get their story straight, then go down and give Jasmine a clean bill of health.

Beau sat down beside his son, cherishing the moment. This was the first time he'd been in his room, and he studied the books and toys arranged on open shelves, trying to understand the child that was part of him.

"Dr. Beau?" Kit hugged a flop-eared stuffed dog in his arms.

"Call me Beau," he whispered.

"Thanks for teaching me to climb the tree. I had fun today."

"It was my pleasure and so did I . . . son."

"I like climbing trees. Can you teach me some other stuff?"

"There's a world of things I want to teach you," he said honestly. If there was anything he knew at this point, it was that he planned to spend a lot of time with his child. "We'll go places and see things. Would you like that?"

A big grin split the small face. "Yeah. Mommy, too?" He yawned despite an obvious effort not to.

"Mommy, too. Go back to sleep, and tomorrow we'll think of something fun to do. Okay?"

"Okay," he said drowsily. Closing his eyes he drifted off to sleep, a faint smile curving his lips.

Beau touched his cheek, marveling at the perfection in the small person who had resulted from the love he and Savanah had shared. His son. He couldn't stop thinking those words.

As a doctor, Beau was acutely aware of the rapid development a child underwent during its first five years, and he felt an overwhelming grief for what he'd missed. He'd missed lying at his wife's side and feeling the exuberant kicking of his unborn child. He'd missed the miracle of birth. Infancy. Toddlerhood. In the fall Kit would start kindergarten, and high school fairly loomed on the horizon.

It was imperative that he not lose another precious moment. He shuddered to think how close he'd come to never knowing Kit even existed. Both he and Savanah had made mistakes, but they weren't irrevocable. The three of them belonged together. Somehow he'd have to make her understand their differences were insignificant compared to the responsibility they had to their child.

He kissed Kit's cheek and pulled the covers up to his chin. He lingered. It was the first time he'd ever tucked his boy into bed, and he wanted to remember the moment forever.

Chapter Six

Beau's first day of pinch-hitting for Doc at the clinic did not begin smoothly. Abner Johnson, confirmed hypochondriac, was the first patient. Doc Ashburton understood the elderly man's preoccupation with an old war injury and prescribed hot-tub soaks to relieve the imaginary pain. He also gave him a bottle of placebos, knowing the kithless old fellow needed the doctor's attention and conversation more than anything medicinal.

But Beau had little patience for Abner, telling him that he was "in very good health for a man his age." He advised Johnson that if he had any discomfort, it was probably due to arthritis and to take ordinary aspirin when it bothered him.

Mr. Johnson left in a huff, mumbling that Doc should've known better than to leave some damn Yankee whipper-snapper in charge. He created quite a disturbance in the waiting room with his vociferous denouncement of Beau's ability.

When they had a minute alone Savanah tore into Beau. "Why did you have to upset Mr. Johnson so much? Doc always gives him a little bottle of sugar pills to satisfy him."

"A man his age doesn't need extra sugar, and it's never wise to encourage healthy people to take up a doctor's time." Beau's chin jutted in determination.

"But Doc would have—"

"I think Doc would want me to use my own judgment."

"I don't think he'd want you to alienate his patients. I'm sure he'll want a practice to return to when his vacation is over," she told him indignantly.

Beau reconsidered. Perhaps it had been a bad call. The purpose of filling in for Doc was to help the old doctor out and satisfy his own professional curiosity about country medicine. Since he'd also like to prove to Savanah that he could fit in if he wanted to, he'd have to remember where he was. "Look," he explained. "I'm accustomed to seeing patients with genuine problems, some of whom had already waited too long before seeking medical treatment. Johnson's trumped-up aches and pains were taking me away from those who might really need help, and it went against my principles to let him do it."

"This isn't Boston, Beau," Savanah reminded him. "The people here have more pedestrian problems than those you're used to treating. Even though Mr. Johnson's case wasn't a life-or-death emergency, he did need something from you."

"There was nothing wrong with him," Beau argued.

"He's an old man with no family and few friends. If you can't see that loneliness is one of his symptoms, maybe you don't belong here."

Maybe he didn't, Beau thought. Small-town tranquility was a nice place to visit, but would he want to live it? Could he ever adjust to a life devoid of the excitement of constant professional challenge? Maybe not, but while he was in Georgia, he'd better do as the Georgians did. Savanah knew more than he about ministering to the needs of the townspeople, and he'd be wise to listen to her.

Before he could respond, she continued, "There are no analysts in Harmony and only one overworked county social worker assigned to this town. Doc understands that his role is to attend not only to his patients' physical needs but to their emotional ones as well. He's mental-health officer, father confessor and physician all in one. You may have to compromise some of your principles if you want to last the duration of Doc's fishing trip."

"I didn't think you wanted me to stay," he said softly. "Why are you trying to help me?"

Savanah had already asked herself that question and hadn't answered it satisfactorily. "I have a responsibility to the patients," she explained. "Doc's counting on us."

"You're right, Savanah. I'll try to adjust my way of thinking while I'm here and work on a whole new set of bedside manners. I'll make a house call later and deliver Johnson's placebo. Will that pacify him?"

"If you eat enough humble pie, it might."

He grinned. "Thanks for setting me straight. Doc told me I could count on you. You may have to bail me out again before the two weeks are up."

"I doubt it, you always were a fast learner."

Later it was Savanah who lost her professional patience. Charity Pickney's appointment was the last before the lunch break, and she monopolized Beau's time with a trumped-up complaint of headaches and fatigue. Her dallying threatened to ruin the tight afternoon scheduling.

Beau was all understanding, just as Savanah had advised him to be, but then he had no way of knowing the woman for what she was. Much to her chagrin, Charity hadn't had a sick day in her life. Doc claimed germs couldn't survive the acidic environment of her personality. She was Harmony's self-appointed town crier and gossip-mill operator. No doubt she'd come in to glean juicy tidbits about Doc's temporary replacement.

Charity would consider it her duty to spread word about the new man in town to all the curious women-folk. Her daughter, Misty Rose, was no doubt the most curious of all.

To her credit, the middle-aged matron tried to live up to her name by joining and subsequently running every noble organization in town. Savanah suspected the woman's efforts weren't strictly altruistic, since her position gave her an inflated sense of self-importance.

When she wasn't spreading rumors Charity's primary occupation was badgering people to volunteer their time for one worthy project or another. It became increasingly obvious that she had an ulterior motive for showing up at the clinic today.

"Well," Charity gushed after her examination. "I know the citizens of Harmony will appreciate any hours you have to spare, Dr. Beaulieu, and I must say I'm duly impressed that you've agreed to spend some of your limited time here to help us out."

Charity batted her eyelashes and continued her rapid-fire dissertation. "I mean, you're practically on vacation even if you are filling in for Doc while he's gone and I'm sure you're a busy man and all, and don't get much time for socializing and here you are, willing to give up a free afternoon to help us raise money for a badly needed playground for the children of Harmony."

Beau was stunned. He'd never heard so many words uttered without benefit of the speaker drawing breath. Mrs. Pickney was a natural for the *Guinness Book of World Records*. When she finally paused, he seized the opportunity to include his nurse in his generous gesture.

"Savanah and I will be happy to volunteer our services at the bazaar." The pink-rinsed blond go-getter had passed her prime, but it was difficult to tell just how long ago that event had taken place. Still she tittered like an adolescent when he winked at her.

Savanah didn't quibble about his generous gesture; she always helped out, anyway. But she had to stare in openmouthed surprise at his next comment.

"I've never worked a kissing booth before, but I'm sure Savanah can give me a few pointers."

They were quickly inked into Charity's little black appointment book and told to report promptly at two o'clock on Sunday. When the elated matron was safely out of earshot, Savanah rounded on Beau. "You have a lot of nerve, Gordon Beaulieu. Just where do you get off volunteering my services?"

"It's for a good cause. As a mother, surely you understand the importance of playgrounds. I couldn't bear to think of my son deprived of swings and slides and monkey bars. It might hinder Kit's development."

"Will you shut up! Charity might still be nosing around and letting her in on a secret is the equivalent of putting up a billboard in the town square."

Beau looked around in mock alarm and pantomimed zipping his lips before laughing at her concern.

"Besides, I always work one of the food booths. Mrs. Pickney's daughter chairs the kissing booth—it's her territory—and we've never gotten along very well." That was putting it delicately. Misty Rose Pickney Clayborne had actively disliked Savanah for years.

It wasn't Savanah's fault Erland Clayborne had asked her to the senior prom first, but it was common knowledge she'd turned him down before he'd eventually gotten around to asking Misty Rose. She wasn't sure if the other woman's resentment stemmed from the fact that Savanah had attracted Erland's attention in the first place, or that she herself hadn't held it.

After all, that date for the prom had led to marriage between the two and a divorce a few years later. Whatever the basis of Misty Rose's aggravation, she harbored a grudge and acted as if her puny divorce settlement was all Savanah's fault.

"It's only one afternoon," Beau was saying. "Surely you can make an effort for such a worthy cause."

"I'd rather make hot dogs in the food booth, it's warmer in there. If the weather changes, we could freeze our lips off."

"Now that would be a pity," he teased. "In the unlikely event a blue northern blows in and spoils the action, I promise to think of something to keep us warm on the job."

"Oh, there'll be plenty of action all right," she muttered, thinking that was exactly what she hated most about the idea. The very thought of him kissing all the women, who would surely be lined up for their chance at the handsome new doctor, made her want to pull someone's hair.

In the days that followed, Savanah and Beau established a good rapport as co-workers. She seemed to anticipate what he needed before he could ask for it, a trait of a skilled and sensitive nurse. He quickly learned to appreciate her way with the patients, and his admiration for her grew.

Pippy and Jasmine had extended him an open invitation to supper anytime he felt like it, and he felt like it all too often. Afterward he'd play with Kit, a new and exciting experience for both of them. The boy was a quick study and was soon climbing trees like a

monkey and sliding down banisters with the grace of
a gymnast.

Sometimes Beau spent the evening on the porch,
rocking in one of the wicker rockers and listening to
the ladies' memories of days gone by. It was during
those time-out periods that he came to truly appreciate small-town life and all it had to offer.

Savanah maneuvered things so that he rarely had a
chance to be alone with her, but she seemed more at
ease in his presence, more willing to accept him into
her daily routine. He was making progress, but beneath the relaxed pleasantries lay a sense of urgency.
Time was running out.

One evening he suggested taking Savanah and Kit
for a ride in his convertible and she agreed, showing
him around town, explaining the historical significance of each landmark and old building.

He found it amazingly easy to slip into the slower
pace of country life and wondered how he'd ever
managed without the simple tranquility. It was trite,
but true, he'd never before taken time to stop and
smell the roses, and he exulted in discovering a world
completely different from the one he'd left in Boston.

He hated when his nightly visits ended, and he had
to return to Doc's house alone. He never had the opportunity to speak to Savanah about any kind of future, and it seemed to him that she carefully avoided
the subject. Neither Pippy nor Jasmine had said a
word about the night of Jasmine's "attack," but they
treated him like a member of the family, clearly assuming things he was afraid to assume.

On the eve of the charity bazaar, Beau and Kit were eating supper in Doc's kitchen, an unexpected concession on Savanah's part. Kit glanced up from spreading peanut butter on bread that was already liberally smeared with grape jelly and marshmallow crème—his personal favorite. "Are you still coming to my birthday party?" he asked hopefully.

"I wouldn't dream of missing it," Beau replied. He planned to give Kit his first two-wheeler, thinking it would be fun to teach him to ride it. "What would you like for a present?"

Kit bit his lip nervously, as though struggling with his conscience over something.

"Come on, tell me the thing you most want," Beau insisted, worried that just because he'd wanted a bike when he was five didn't mean his son did.

The boy shrugged, grinning shyly.

Beau's smile was indulgent. Good breeding at work again. Kit was too shy to speak up and ask for what he wanted. "I want to give you a special present, because you're…my special friend. So tell me what you want."

"You mean what I want most in the whole wide world?"

"That's what I mean."

"Well, what I want most, more than anything, is for you to take me fishing."

"Fishing?" Beau repeated. "Just fishing?"

"Yeah." Kit sighed. "All the other kids go fishing and camping with their daddies, and I don't have nobody to take me. Mommy said you're too busy for that stuff, but I told her we're friends, and you said that friends ain't never too busy for each other."

"That's right. Friends *aren't* ever too busy for one another. What did she say to that?"

"She said not to ask you. But we don't have to go camping, Beau, just fishing's okay. I've never been before. Could we go? We don't have to stay real long."

Beau poured Kit a glass of milk and fell in love with his son all over again. He'd do anything to see that bright light of enthusiasm on his child's face. "I think we can arrange that. If your mom gives her permission, that is." It galled him to have to qualify his promise, but Savanah would have to be consulted.

"Gosh, Beau, do you have to tell her I asked you?" Kit said with a worried frown creasing his tiny brow.

Beau laughed heartily. "No, I think I can convince her that it was all my idea." Kit looked relieved and began munching on his sloppy sandwich. "Why don't you have some ham with that gooey mess of yours?"

"Okay," Kit agreed amiably. "I'll just have what you're havin'."

During the first week of Beau's visit Savanah came to regret that she'd never forged any strong feminine friendships. She had plenty of acquaintances and was on speaking terms with just about everyone in town, but there was no special friend she could confide in, and she felt the lack sorely.

She was more confused than ever about her feelings for Beau, and what was happening between them. It would have been wonderful to have someone with more sophistication in the ways of men than the precious little she possessed with whom to discuss the matter.

Her mother would give the situation a fair hearing, but then she'd probably tell her to follow her heart and do whatever she thought best. Good advice in itself, but she didn't believe what her heart was telling her, and she certainly didn't know what was best. She felt her mother was too far away and too preoccupied with her own life to be bothered. This was something she'd just have to sort out on her own.

She'd grown lax in monitoring the time Beau spent with Kit. At first she worried that Beau wouldn't take his responsibility seriously enough. She feared his interest in Kit was merely that of a man who'd suddenly discovered he was a parent and once the novelty had worn off, so would his curiosity. For once she was glad to be wrong.

Beau *had* matured since they'd parted, and it was clear his fondness for Kit was genuine. And the feelings were mutual. The fact that Kit was becoming attached to Beau worried her, but given the circumstances she couldn't find it in her heart to stand between them. Perhaps the greatest gift she could ever give her son was his father.

She suffered no delusions where she and Beau were concerned. Eventually they'd have to go their separate ways. The lure of the big city would summon him home sooner or later. He might pretend to enjoy sitting on the veranda and swapping tales with Jasmine and Pippy, but he would come to realize that there was nothing to challenge him in Harmony.

He was doing fairly well at the clinic, considering the fact that he was an "outsider" and a Yankee to boot. Even those who came to him expecting to dislike him were eventually won over by his sincerity and charm.

She hadn't thought he'd put forth so much effort or try so hard. But he had a passion for medicine that matched all his other passions, and he put his patients first. The time would come when he would have to take his gift where it could best serve others—to a big city. His time in Harmony was just a pleasant diversion.

So no matter how many ways she looked at things, no matter how many times she put the pieces together, they always made up the same picture. She wouldn't be happy in Boston, and Beau wouldn't be happy if he didn't return. Someone had to think logically and it wouldn't be him, he was too passionate to think about practical manners. She had to maintain some emotional distance to keep from being hurt all over again.

She still cared, she realized with a knifing pain. Time had changed nothing in that regard. When she was with him it was as if the years rolled away, and she was that same giddy, young girl who'd loved unwisely before.

She'd fought it, even tried to deny it, but in those still-of-the-night moments when she was forced to be honest with herself, she could admit she still had a grand desire for Gordon Beaulieu. When reality interceded, she told herself that desire wasn't enough.

There had to be shared goals, values and dreams. She and Beau simply didn't have the same dreams.

The weather cooperated on the day of the fundraiser. The sun shone brightly, and a slight breeze carried the sweet green scent of spring. The decorated booths set up in the park were crowded with people intent upon having a good time and spending their money. Tinny music swelled from a small carousel, competing with the fiddlers and banjo players in the bandstand.

Deciding a demure look appropriate for kissing-booth duty, Savanah changed from her church suit into a calf-length challis skirt in a rich burgundy print. With it she wore a white blouse with a portrait collar, and a burgundy sleeveless cotton-sweater vest. Knowing she would be on her feet, she'd worn flat-heeled shoes that made her feel even smaller than usual as she stood at Beau's side.

Business at the kissing booth had been slow when they arrived, but it picked up when the ladies caught sight of Beau. He looked so handsome and kissable in his chocolate-brown corduroy slacks and bulky, cream-colored sweater. Its V-neck allowed a discreet amount of chest hair to peek out invitingly and was calculated to beckon female hands to touch. Savanah wondered if the ladies of Harmony would have trouble obeying the rule against any physical contact other than primly pursed lips.

Hands could definitely be a problem, she decided, especially her own. She'd always known Beau was a handsome man, but she hadn't realized just how dangerously exciting he was until she'd seen him mingling with ordinary mortals. She was studying him so intently that she was startled when he spoke.

"You look sweet today. But that outfit won't lure in many unsuspecting customers," Beau teased.

"It wasn't meant to," she informed him, thinking about how alluring he was. She'd have to watch it; she was on the verge of offering to be a customer herself. There was poetic justice, she thought. He'd been the first man for her, hadn't he? He'd been the only man, and he'd always be the only... She had to stop thinking like that, since she was in imminent danger of having another hot flashback.

"It's a beautiful day for it." He grinned down at her, wondering if she would object to kissing him in the name of charity if he gave her a dollar. She was skittish, he noted, so perhaps he'd better not offer.

"A beautiful day for what?" Savanah asked, lost in her own fantasy world.

"Anything," he replied. "But since it's for a good cause and spring is the season that turns young men's fancies, let's hope it'll be a beautiful day for kissing."

"Indeed." She groaned. "Get your pucker ready."

"Why?"

"Don't look now, but here comes Misty Rose Clayborne, the fastest lips in the South. Don't be surprised if she says something nasty to me, she's reliable that way."

"Well, well, who do we have here? The charmin' new doctor, no doubt...Savanah dear, introduce us properly now. Won't you?" The blonde purred.

Savanah's smile was as false as it was bright. "Hello, Misty Rose. Are you sure you want to use propriety here?" she drawled, mockingly.

Misty Rose's laugh was completely artificial, and the way she tossed back her hair seemed staged, as if she practiced in front of a mirror. "Well, I'll forgive you if you can't manage it . . . everyone knows you're anything but proper."

Although she'd started it this time, Savanah tired of the slam game first, probably because she knew she'd never get the best of her skilled opponent. "Dr. Gordon Beaulieu, this is Misty Rose Clayborne," she introduced ungraciously, thinking it would be kinder to toss him into a pool of hungry piranhas.

"It's such a pleasure to finally meet ya'," Misty Rose gushed. "Mama told me all about you, and I've been looking forward to it for simply days."

"My pleasure." Beau smiled a greeting.

Savanah's attention was claimed by Roy Lee Whitaker, junior high-school football coach and town Lothario. Harmony wasn't cosmopolitan enough to support a full-time gigolo, but Roy Lee did his best. His reputation as a ladies' man was largely self-enhanced, but he seemed to believe his own publicity.

He'd asked Savanah out a number of times, and she'd always turned him down. However, Roy Lee was the type who figured any woman who didn't fall for him surely had a problem that, given the opportunity, he could cure. "Hello, you purty little peach blossom," he boomed. "Does this here sign mean I have to pay for your kisses today?"

There wasn't enough money south of the Mason-Dixon line for him to buy her kisses, Savanah thought uncharitably.

Beau lost interest in Misty Rose at about the same time Savanah stopped listening to their conversation. He nodded a lot, shrugged occasionally, and attentively ignored what the bottle blonde had to say. He was tuned into the conversation beside him.

Savanah wanted to scream when Roy Lee placed a bill on the counter between them. "You really gonna charge ole Roy Lee for a few kisses?"

She'd sworn that the only way her lips would touch his was in the event he required resuscitation—and even then she'd have to think about it. Her smile barely escaped becoming a grimace. "That's what the sign says."

"Well then, sugar, I want five dollars worth." Roy Lee leered and grabbed her in a bruising grip, pulling her chest to his. So much for the rule about nothing physical. When his hard lips clamped down on hers, she thought she'd gag, but rolling her eyes toward Beau made her feel a little better. If it had been summer, he could have caught a few flies in his open-mouthed astonishment.

Beau endured the travesty as long as he could bear before thumping Roy Lee on the shoulder. "Your five dollars are up, big guy." Something suspiciously like jealousy made him want to smash his fist into the man's previously broken nose.

Roy Lee released Savanah, then turned his most intimidating look on Beau. It was the one he used to control his team of fractious fourteen-year-olds. "I didn't hear the lady doin' any complainin'."

"Maybe because you never let her up for air," Beau said with deadly calm. "It's hard to talk when you're caught in a lip-lock."

"Now, Roy Lee," Misty Rose cajoled. "If you want more kissin', you'll just have to pay for it. This is for charity, ya' know."

"That's right." Knowing what a tightwad he was, Savanah felt relatively secure in agreeing.

"Well then, I reckon I'll just have to go cash a check since I used up all my cash on the basketball throw." He turned to leave, assuring Savanah over his shoulder, "Don't you worry none, honey, I'll be back. Keep your motor runnin'."

"Don't you worry, buddy," Beau smirked. "I'll see if I can't rev it up a little while you're gone."

Savanah laughed.

Misty Rose glowered. "Am I goin' to be forced to take my money elsewhere?" she whined, waving a twenty.

Savanah sobered instantly, angry that she found the thought of Beau kissing Misty Rose so disturbing. "No. I'm sure Dr. Beaulieu can quite happily accommodate you."

Savanah's apparent indifference brought Beau's chin up in a challenge. "Your money is always good here, ma'am," he said.

It was clear Misty Rose intended to single-handedly pay for the new playground equipment, but Savanah didn't have to stand idly by and watch the proceedings. Luckily, Kit chose that moment to hit her up for some money.

"I spent all my quarters, Mommy."

She dug into her wallet and handed him some change. "Let me know when you need more, sweetie. Where's Pippy and Aunt Jasmine?"

"Here comes Auntie Jasmine now. I think Granny Pip is in the confession tent," Kit announced.

Jasmine giggled and fluttered her ever-present hanky. "Kit, darlin', that's *concession* tent."

Beau laughed between kisses, and Misty Rose told him to keep his mind on his work.

Jasmine giggled, and Savanah had to suppress the urge to laugh at the predicament he'd gotten himself into. Kit frowned and asked, "Mommy, why's Dr. Beau kissin' Miz Clayborne?"

"Some people will do anything for money, dear," she said airily, with a pointed, distasteful look.

Misty Rose winked at Beau and whispered something for his ears only, before disappearing into the crowd.

Savanah sighed dramatically, "I do hope I didn't run her off," she lied.

"I think she ran out of money," he said.

"Where's she off to? Gone to mortgage her house?"

Beau smiled knowingly. "Gee, I didn't know you cared."

"What you do and who you kiss is your own business."

"I was hoping you'd consider it yours, under the circumstances."

"And what circumstances are those, pray tell?" she asked with mock indifference.

"Misty Rose just claimed several dances with me tonight at her mother's 'après-bazaar' festivities. I thought you might have some objections to that as well."

"I have no objections if you don't. Everybody says Misty Rose is the best dancer in town. The prettiest, too. Even her name is pretty."

"It might have suited her when she was a fresh-faced child, but the years have sort of dried the dew off the flower. Just imagine calling her that forty years from now."

"I imagine folks'll be calling her Musty Rose by then," Savanah declared cattily.

Beau smiled. "Thanks for bailing me out. I owe you one."

"Consider us even, you got rid of Roy Lee, didn't you?"

"Yes, but he's coming back."

"If he comes back, I'll hide under the counter and you can kiss him."

"I'm going to get you for that," he said menacingly.

"Kit, would you like to ride the carousel with me? I think we are definitely *de trop* here," Aunt Jasmine interjected.

Savanah grabbed her handbag, flipped back the counter and stepped out of the booth. "I'm going with you," she said with a just-you-try-to-stop-me smirk in Beau's direction.

He shrugged, looked unconcerned and glanced at his watch. The next kissers would relieve them in ten minutes, anyway. It was a small place—he'd find her. "See ya' later," he drawled in warning.

Not if I see you first, she thought.

Savanah waved to Kit each time he made the circuit on the merry-go-round. She'd just leaned back on the bench, making herself comfortable, when two hands covered her eyes.

"Guess who?"

"Mel Gibson?" she asked hopefully.

Beau removed his hands and plopped down beside her. "Is that who you were waiting for?"

"I gave up waiting for him years ago. There's only one man in my life now."

Beau grinned and sat up a little taller. "Do I know him?"

"Of course you do. He's the one on the blue pony."

"What about Crazy Lips Whitaker?"

"Roy Lee? You've got to be kidding."

"Have there been any other men in your life, Savanah?"

Beau's question came out of nowhere, and she gave him a sidelong glance. "What are you asking exactly?"

His hand clutched hers on the bench between them. "I'm asking if there's ever been another man in your life."

"What you really want to know is whether or not I've ever made love to another man, isn't that it?" She didn't like conducting such a private conversation in such a public place.

Beau brought her hand to his lips and kissed it. "Both. I admit it bothers me to think of you with anyone else. I still want you and that hasn't changed. At night I lie awake, and all I can think of is how wonderful it would be to hold you, to make love to you."

Savanah glanced around to make sure no one had seen his covetous gesture before slipping her hand out of his. "If that's true, it's only because you can't have me."

"Maybe, but it doesn't change the fact that I want you and need you. Regardless of the reasons."

"Beau, I feel very uncomfortable sitting here on a park bench, discussing wants and needs with you. It's hardly the place."

Kit's ride was over and he ran up, waving and calling, "Hey, Mommy. Hey, Beau."

The intense mood was broken, and Beau grinned at his son, thinking romance was difficult with children around to complicate it. "Speaking of wants, Kit and I want to go fishing," he said, pulling the boy onto his lap.

Savanah laughed. "I think fishing falls into the fondest-wish category."

"If it's all right with you, I'd like to take him over to Cletus Tyrell's pond some evening. Want to come along?"

She almost said yes. No matter how hard she tried to avoid him, no matter how much distance she put between them, she wanted nothing more than a few stolen moments with Beau. Then she saw Kit's face.

He was trying to put on his 'Sure Mom, why dontcha come?' expression but was failing. She recognized his need to be alone with Beau, man to man, was greater than her own and couldn't bring herself to intrude on that special time. "I'm not much of a fishing fan. You guys go on. If you catch some, I'll help you eat them, though."

"Yippee!" Kit bounced on Beau's lap. "When do we go?"

"Tomorrow. That is, if we can find the gear we need."

"No problem. Granny Pip's got about a jillion fishin' poles."

Digging into his pocket for change, Beau handed Kit a quarter. "Want to ride the merry-go-round again?"

There was no such thing as too many rides on the carousel and Kit happily skipped away. When the music started up Beau turned to Savanah. "I've been thinking about taking Kit to Stone Mountain. Do you think he'd like it?"

"Well, I don't know," she pretended to consider. "Little boys aren't too wild about theme parks."

"Will you go with us? It would mean a lot to me for us to have some time alone as a family before I leave."

So he *was* leaving. She'd known it was inevitable, but it hurt to hear him say it. "Sure. It might be good for you two to spend some time together. Kit's birthday party is Friday, but you can take him over the weekend."

She'd ignored the fact that his invitation included her. "I want you to come with us."

"Don't you think you'd have more fun if you just took Kit?" Savanah's heart was beating too fast. She'd been telling herself that Beau's primary interest was in his son, and she was giving him an easy out. She waited to see if he'd jump at the chance.

"No. I said I wanted us to have some time together as a family."

"But we aren't a family. What's the point in pretending we are?"

"There's nothing wrong with pretending," Beau said softly. "When I was Kit's age I believed if I wanted something badly enough, all I had to do was pretend it was so."

"You're a big boy now," she said with a nervous laugh. "Surely you've outgrown that pointless fantasy."

He turned away from her and waved at Kit, who was making yet another circuit. "Fantasy is never pointless," he said with a sigh. "Sometimes it's absolutely necessary."

Chapter Seven

Beau was right. Sometimes fantasy *was* necessary, Savanah admitted grudgingly as she parked in front of the Pickney house. It was by far the grandest in Harmony and topped a small rise just outside of town. She helped Pippy and Jasmine out of the car and thought it was certainly a fantasy that she was going to enjoy this little extravaganza. She was already experiencing a feeling of trepidation that only a trip to the gallows should inspire.

Did she care that Misty "Clinging Vine" Clayborne had staked Beau out as personal territory? No one else in Harmony knew that Savanah was married to Beau, nor would they ever know. She could act as cool as the next estranged wife, couldn't she?

Maybe she'd even do a bit of flirting herself. That should convince Beau she was totally unaffected by him. Theirs was a marriage in name only and would soon be over, as proved by his announcement that he'd be leaving shortly. Obtaining a legal divorce was the next logical step to dissolving a relationship that had been doomed from the start.

Beau groaned inwardly when he saw Misty Rose swishing through the crowd with two cups of fruit punch held aloft. The chiffon-swathed blonde left little doubt as to her plans to appropriate him, she'd been broadcasting her intentions across the room for the past few minutes. He smiled pleasantly, but hoped not too encouragingly, in return.

"Why, here you are, Dr. Beaulieu," she drawled, handing him a crystal cup of punch he didn't want. "Shall I call you Gordon? Formal address just doesn't seem appropriate somehow after our sojourn in the kissing booth."

"You may certainly call me Gordon," he said, without adding that Christine, his mother and her servants were the only ones who ever had.

"I can't tell you how fortunate we are to have you here in Harmony, Gordon. Why, I shudder to think what would've happened to poor Mother if you hadn't been there to save her. The thought just gives me cold chills." To prove the point, Misty Rose shivered, inviting the good doctor to comfort her with more than words.

Beau attempted to minimize his part in the little drama that had unfolded in the concession tent just before the bazaar was over. While he was there, having a soft drink, Charity Pickney had choked on a corn dog, and he'd saved her with an expertly applied Heimlich maneuver. A large crowd, gathered to take advantage of half-priced refreshments, had witnessed the off-duty feat, and he'd risen several notches in the estimation of the townspeople.

"Anyone could have done what I did. I just happened to be handy."

"Now, don't be so modest, it's a poor dog who won't wag his own tail," she chided. "You were coolheaded and fast thinking. I just love a fast-thinking man. Anyway, your actions were quite heroic. Everybody says so." She took a coy sip of punch and peered up at him through heavily mascaraed lashes.

"Thank you," he responded, it was useless to argue with her. He listened with one ear while the woman prattled on, all the while watching and listening for Savanah's arrival. Time was running out, and he was no closer to changing her mind about the divorce than when he'd first approached her. She was as stubborn as any woman could get.

This afternoon the Magnolia Brigade had sought him out covertly, practically hijacking him behind the handicrafts booth. They had demanded to know whether or not his intentions toward Savanah were honorable, and he'd assured them that they were. His primary problem, he'd explained, was convincing Savanah. He'd wanted to tell the older women that the annulment was nonexistent, but he'd promised Savanah he wouldn't divulge that secret just yet.

It had taken some talking to convince them of his good intentions, but by the time the unscheduled meeting was over, he'd won their approval and support. In the end they'd smiled and told him not to worry, they were on his side. It was their contention that true love wills out in the end.

He didn't doubt that what he felt for Savanah was "true love" and he would never let another woman into his heart—not after the way Savanah had trampled it by leaving him.

As for Kit, the boy had carved a niche for himself in Beau's heart, and there he would always stay, no matter what.

Beau saw the trio come in and grinned. Misty Rose followed his glance and quickly turned back to him as if Savanah's entrance weren't worthy of comment. "As I was sayin'..." she continued her monologue about the cultural advantages to be enjoyed in Atlanta.

Beau wasn't listening. He was totally entranced by Savanah who wore a form-fitting blue silk dress the exact color of her eyes. The surplice top emphasized her modest bosom and the wrapped skirt displayed her tiny waist to perfection.

Despite the worried crease on her brow, she was the most attractive woman present, and Beau would be proud to proclaim her as his wife in any gathering. As soon as Misty Rose came up for air, he'd excuse himself and tell Savanah just how lovely she was.

"Why hello, sugar, you're a vision," boomed an unfortunately familiar voice.

Savanah tried to arrange her features appropriately before turning her attention to the owner of the twangy barritone. "Thank you, Roy Lee," she said flatly. She suffered no delusions that he'd actually get the message her unenthusiastic response was meant to convey.

"How-do, Miz Jefferson, Miz Potter? Are you charmin' ladies without benefit of an escort this evening?" His words included all of them, but his eyes were for Savanah only.

Jasmine took the initiative. "Much to our regret, dear boy, we are. And we're fairly parched. Would you be so kind as to fetch us some of that sumptuous-looking punch?"

He hesitated as if unwilling to leave Savanah long enough to run such an errand. But his mama had instilled some manners in him, including respect for his elders. He agreed reluctantly, "Why surely, Miz Jefferson. It'd be a pleasure."

"You're a sweet boy to do it," Pippy muttered. Under her breath she added, "And take your time."

Though not in a partying mood, Savanah decided to mingle. She could see what Beau was up to and escape Roy Lee's sweaty clutches at the same time. She wandered into what Charity ambitiously called the music room, and her ear tuned into Beau's distinctive accent before she actually saw him.

Her hungry gaze sought him out. She hadn't seen him dressed up in a long time, and the sight nearly took her breath away. He wore a lightweight, cream-colored suit, a smoky blue shirt and a subtly striped tie. He was so handsome it made her stomach ache to watch him with Misty Rose.

Dr. Heartbreak rides again. Savanah was suddenly awash with memories. The first time she'd ever seen him was at a crowded party such as this. He'd looked

just as devastating then, but maturity had given him a
more intensely masculine assurance. He fairly vi-
brated blatant sexuality.

Savanah really was parched, and it had nothing to
do with thirst. Thinking about Beau and their previ-
ous relationship had elevated her temperature. She felt
an embarrassing flush threaten her cheeks. That old
feeling started tingling at the core of her being, radi-
ating upward and outward, until even her fingertips
stung with anticipation.

She had to regain her composure. It wouldn't do to
have such thoughts while he was in the same room and
with so many people present. She turned away from
the distressing sight of him and mechanically made her
way to the refreshment table. She wasn't sure she could
swallow around the lump in her throat, but toying with
a punch cup would give her something to do with her
hands.

"Allow me," came the seductively whispered command. Savanah spun around and practically stepped
into Beau's arms.

"I can pour my own punch," she said defensively.

"I keep forgetting. You don't need a man for anything."

"Not anymore, I don't," she said breezily. She
started to walk away, but his hand on her arm de-
tained her.

"Isn't there anything I can do for you, Savanah,
that you can't do for yourself?" His hand gently caressed her arm, and she fought the impulse to challenge him by throwing herself on him and doing
something inappropriate before mixed company.

"If it's a helpless female you want, Misty Rose is a better choice."

"Cut it out. You know I'm not interested in her or anyone else for that matter. What do I have to do to convince you that you're the woman I want?"

"Lower your voice," she commanded, checking to see if that unpropitious remark had been overheard above what purported to be a Mozart concerto that the church organist was improvising. "Do you want people to hear you?"

"As a matter of fact, I do. I think it's time the whole world knew that you're my wife, Savanah Winslow Beaulieu."

"Really, Beau," she said in exasperation. "Will you hush?"

"Maybe what I need to do," he said with a sweeping gesture, "is tell this gentle assemblage the whole story. I'll bet the majority of those present respect the sanctity of marriage and believe a wife should cleave only unto her husband. What do you think?"

"I think you're crazy. There's no need to air our emotional laundry in front of half the town."

"How long are you going to punish me for not coming after you six years ago?"

"I'm doing no such thing."

"What is it, then? I know what you need, what we both need." He tugged her close. "I see it in your eyes when you look at me. I feel it in the tremor of your body when I hold you."

"Stop it. You're creating a scene." She was frantic with embarrassment and desire and tried to wiggle from his grasp without attracting undue attention.

"Then step out to the terrace with me, and we'll conclude this discussion in private. God knows, you haven't let yourself be alone with me all week. What are you afraid of?" he whispered, his face too close to hers.

"I'm not afraid of anything, and this conversation is over."

"Is that what you think?"

"That's what I know." Savanah wheeled away from him and accidently set up a collision course with Roy Lee. He leered at her, waving for her to wait for him. She pivoted around, hoping to appear as if she hadn't seen him, and ran smack-dab into Beau.

She didn't need this.

"Looks like your choice is clear," he whispered in her ear. "Who will it be? Me or Roy Lee?"

What had she ever done to deserve this? Hadn't she paid dearly enough for being a foolish, lovesick girl? Although she'd never really gotten over Beau, she'd reached the point where she didn't yearn for him at least a hundred times a day. And she no longer woke up crying for him in the night.

Life had actually become bearable. But now looking at him, her wounds tore open afresh and the hot fever stirred her blood. She wanted to touch him, to feel his lips on hers, to press her naked body against his. She couldn't give in, however, no matter how badly she wanted to.

She considered her options and decided that fighting off Beau on the terrace was preferable to fighting off that leech, Roy Lee, anywhere. Grabbing Beau's arm, she dragged him across the crowded room and the surprised guests parted like the Red Sea.

"Come on. If you're so intent on getting me alone, let's have at it," she snapped.

"I love it when you get all aggressive," he teased when they'd gained the privacy of the terrace.

"Oh, you do, do you?"

"Yeah. Say, could you manhandle me a little more? I kind of enjoyed that."

"Gordon Beaulieu, you're pressing the limits of my patience," she said through clenched teeth.

"I'd rather be pressing your soft body beneath mine."

"Don't say things like that!" She covered her ears with her hands; the man had somehow read her thoughts.

"Why not?" he asked innocently. "You're my wife. Marital body pressing can't be a totally new concept on this side of the Mason-Dixon line."

"What do you want from me?" she asked in frustration.

"I thought I'd made that pretty clear, but evidently there's been a breakdown in communications." He pulled her against him and molded her body to his with both palms. His hands skated up and down her back, and the filmy material of her dress provided little protection from the sparks his touch ignited.

His hands slipped lower, cupping her softly rounded backside, and a soft moan escaped her when she felt the unmistakable heat of his arousal. He was definitely communicating now.

"Oh, Savanah, do you have any idea how crazy I've been with wanting you? I watch your window every night, and when your light goes out I picture you undressing and getting into bed. Then I remember how it was when I was there beside you, kissing you." He matched actions to words. "Touching you." He sought her breast, and its soft weight filled his hand. "Loving you." His hips ground gently against hers. "I have almost total recall, but it isn't quite good enough."

His lips claimed hers in a consuming kiss. "Remember what I said about wanting something so much that you make it happen?"

She gasped for breath as if she'd just been dragged from a drowning pool. "Do you remember what I said about there being no future for us?"

He nuzzled her neck, nipping her ear tenderly. "No. My recall is also selective."

"You're impossible."

"Not at all. Just whisper a few sweet nothings in my ear and I'll melt like butter on a hot griddle." He proceeded to demonstrate what he had in mind.

Savanah felt like laughing at his outrageous antics. He always had been able to make her laugh, even when she didn't want to. But she had to remember that he was nothing but a pushy Yankee who had never taken no for an answer in his life. This was one time he would have to. She reminded herself that his true goal in all this heavy wooing was her son. He was totally unprincipled and would go to any lengths to assure his place in Kit's life.

"Look Beau, I've been thinking."

"Don't think, just feel."

"Will you stop licking my ear so I can talk to you?"

"I wasn't licking," he defended. "I was nibbling."

"Well, stop that, too. I've come to the conclusion that you would make a good father for Kit."

"That's reassuring to hear. It's a little difficult to undo these things once they've been done."

"I mean, I think Kit needs his father. It's clear you love him, and that he loves you."

"He needs a mother and a father, he'll have both."

"I agree." She tried to make herself aloof. "So, I have a proposition for you."

"No need to trouble yourself. I'm easy."

"Will you shut up and be serious? I'm trying to say that if you want to tell Kit you're his father, I think it will be all right now. I believe he's ready for it. I'll try to explain everything the best I can. At his age he probably won't have that many questions. He'll be so excited to find out he has a father, he won't even wonder why we didn't tell him before."

"Do you really believe that?"

"No, but allow me my illusions. This is hard enough without you making it worse. I won't fight you about visitation. We can alternate holidays, and you can have him in Boston for a month each summer." It was more than she'd been prepared to offer, and yet she knew it wasn't nearly enough.

The smile faded from Beau's face. "You're serious about this, aren't you?"

"Dead."

"I don't want to be a father with visitation privileges. I think we should try to be a family. A real fam-

ily whose members care for one another. I want Kit to
have security, maybe even the brothers and sisters I
never had. It's not right to shuffle children back and
forth between parents. Believe me, I know what it's
like. You don't have two homes, you have none, and
it's a damnable feeling to think you don't really belong in either. I don't want that for my son.''

Beau's words strengthened her resolve. He didn't
want a wife, he wanted a mother for his child. ''It
must have been hard for you. But it doesn't have to be
that way for Kit. If you want a role in his life, you'll
have to take my offer because it's all I can willingly
give.''

''It isn't entirely for you to decide.'' His dark eyes
bored into hers as if to control her.

''You can't make me live with you. But you do have
a choice about how difficult you make the divorce.''

''I won't give up.'' He stared at her with the determination of an outnumbered marine. ''I'll be here
another week, and a lot can happen in seven days.''

''Beau, you're wasting your time.''

''I'll be the judge of that. Let's hold off telling Kit
until after the Stone Mountain trip. Okay?''

''Okay.''

When he swooped down for a hard possessive kiss,
she allowed herself the luxury of not resisting. She'd
made up her mind and no amount of sensual assault
was going to change it. She felt that no matter how
much he claimed to want her, he would never love her.
He'd mentioned desire, passion, wants and needs—
but never love, which was what she needed to hear.

If he professed love now, she still wouldn't be convinced. There was no way he could prove his desire wasn't just a ricochet of his intense feelings for Kit.

So she returned what she considered a farewell kiss, and when he released her she rounded up Pippy and Jasmine to go home. She had to get away from the tantalizing but pointless feelings Beau aroused in her, away from his tempting kisses and persuasive words.

As the coil of unfulfilled desire tightened within her, she fought to cling to reality. Fantasy be damned.

The hectic schedule of the next week kept Savanah and Beau too busy to think about themselves. First, Junior Carver lost three fingers of his right hand in an accident at the sawmill. He and the severed digits were rushed to the clinic and Beau called for a medical helicopter to airlift the injured man to a hospital in Atlanta.

The specialist in charge made it clear that if not for Beau's medical skill Junior's fingers could not have been successfully reattached. The prognosis for Junior was good, and he was expected to regain limited use of his hand.

The patient's grateful young wife wasted no time in letting the community know how lucky they were to have the services, even temporarily, of such a talented doctor. Her praise added to Beau's reputation, which was already enhanced by Charity Pickney's rigid insistence that she wouldn't be alive if it weren't for him.

The dust had barely settled when a teenage boy was brought into the clinic suffering severe abdominal pain. Beau removed the ruptured appendix before transferring the boy to the hospital. He and Savanah supervised the ambulance technicians, making sure their young patient was comfortable, before watching the vehicle drive out of sight.

"Good job, Doctor," she complimented.

"Country medicine is turning out to be more than just treating hay fever," he said with a sigh.

"We have our share of emergencies. Doc's been at it for more than forty years, and he claims to have seen it all. You can understand why he needed a vacation."

Big drops of rain began to fall as they turned to go inside. "It's past office hours. Let's lock it up and call it a day."

He turned and smiled at her. "We may be in for quite a storm. There's some nasty-looking clouds off to the north." Beau stood in the open doorway and watched the rain pelt the dusty street. The sky had taken on a foreboding darkness, and clouds now obscured the late afternoon sun.

"They do look bad," she agreed. "I hope Pippy doesn't try to drive home in it."

She and Jasmine had taken Kit into Atlanta for a day of birthday shopping and had promised him dinner at his favorite fast-food restaurant before starting home. It unnerved Savanah to think of the old lady driving in this downpour.

"I'm sure she'll see fit to wait it out." He didn't dare tell her just how sure he was. "You'll get soaked if you go home now. Is there any chance at all you'd stay and make me one of those 'anything goes' omelets I remember so well? We can listen to the weather reports on the radio.''

She agreed reluctantly. They didn't need the intimacy a shared supper and thunderstorm could provide. She'd grown close to Beau while working at his side the past few days and knew it was asking for trouble to spend the evening with him. Still, the prospect of sitting out the storm alone and waiting for word from her family made her uneasy and she relented.

The telephone rang as they were finishing their omelets. It was Pippy, informing Savanah that they wouldn't be coming home. Atlanta was in the center of the storm, and they'd made arrangements to spend the night with a friend. Kit was fine, she assured. He was excited by the prospect of a little adventure. Reports said the storm would blow itself out by morning, and they'd be home in plenty of time for Kit's afternoon birthday party.

When she related this to Beau he nodded and agreed to the wisdom of the decision. Secretly, however, he was curious. At their last strategy meeting, Pippy and Jasmine had assured him they would manage to arrange some time for him to be alone with Savanah. What he wanted to know was how the old connivers had managed to brew up a storm of such epic proportions.

They were in Doc's old-fashioned kitchen, washing dishes, when someone pounded on the door. Beau opened it, and Savanah peered around him at the unfamiliar young man who was quickly becoming soaked.

"Are you the doctor?" he asked breathlessly. "The guy at the gas station said there was a doctor here."

"I'm Dr. Beaulieu, come in out of the rain."

He shook his head. "It's my wife. I think she's gone into early labor. She needs help."

Within minutes they had Betsy Crawford, a frightened young mother-to-be, settled on an examining table in the clinic. After Beau's examination, he spoke to her gently and reassured her that while everything was fine, her baby was about to make his debut a bit ahead of schedule.

"It's my fault, isn't it?" she implored. "I never should have taken this trip. It's just that my daddy had a heart attack, and I had to see him. Will all this traveling hurt the baby?"

"No. You have nothing to worry about. You mustn't blame yourself," Beau told her. "Even if you'd spent the last month of your pregnancy in your own living room, Junior might have decided to come early. It appears he's the impatient type."

"Do you think it's a boy, Doctor?"

"We'll know soon enough." Beau motioned Savanah into the next room. After assuring Betsy she'd be right back, she joined him. "How long will it be, do you think?"

"That's a tough call. She's already dilated to seven, that's why I didn't send them on to the hospital. But it's her first pregnancy, so it's hard to say. My professional opinion, since I'm not an obstetrician, may be off. But I think we'll see a baby in an hour or so."

A moan from the other room ended the discussion.

Much later, Jim Crawford took Beau aside. "You can tell me the truth, Doc. It's been three hours. What's the matter?" He raked his hand through hair that was already badly disheveled. His eyes were as wide and frightened as his young wife's. "Is anything going to happen to Betsy?"

Beau put his hand on the young man's shoulder in a reassuring manner and said firmly, "No. We're not going to let it. These things just take time, we can't rush them."

"I shouldn't have let her take this trip. But the baby wasn't due for almost a month, and she wanted to see her daddy."

"I know it's difficult, but all we can do is wait." Savanah sympathized. "Try not to worry. Dr. Beaulieu's a fine physician, and he'll bring your child into the world safely. Why don't you go in and sit with her for a while?" she suggested gently.

"Nurse," came a feeble cry, and Savanah hurried back to her vigil at Betsy's side.

"She's right," Beau told Jim. "Betsy needs you."

"I can't go back in there. I can't stand to see her suffer. Isn't there something you can give her?"

"It would be dangerous to give her any drugs at this point. She's very close to delivery. What she needs now is you. Your support is the best medicine she can get."

"But it's terrible to see her in pain. Her suffering, it's all my fault. I didn't think it'd be like this, that it'd hurt so much to have a baby."

"Beau." Savanah's head appeared around the door. "It's about time."

"Come on, Jim."

"I can't go in there, I feel sick."

Beau grasped the young man's shirtfront. "She needs you, Jim, and you need to be with her when your child is born. It's one of the most important moments in your lives. Believe me, if you don't go in there, you'll regret it. I didn't have the chance to be with my wife when our son was born, and for that I'll be eternally sorry. Now, come on, Papa."

Savanah had coached Betsy through the various breathing techniques required to insure a smooth delivery. As a result, the young woman was alert and in control of her pain, though visibly fatigued. It was nearly over, and her husband's encouragement was helping her through the most difficult stage.

"You're doing great, Betsy," Savanah enthused during a strong contraction. "Just keep panting until Dr. Beau tells you the baby's ready. It won't be much longer."

"But I'm so tired," she sighed weakly.

"Of course you are," Savanah replied gently. "You've been working very hard. That's why they call it labor."

"I don't think I can last much longer, Savanah." The young woman's face was slick with sweat and pinched from her ordeal.

"Yes, you can. Give me your hand and let's breathe into the next one together."

Working diligently at the other end of the table, Beau finally gave the magic command. "Push!" he instructed the exhausted but now impatient Betsy. She followed his directives to the letter, and two pushes later Beau triumphantly introduced the new mother to her squirming, screaming, battle-weary baby boy.

"Oh, Jimmy," Betsy cried to her husband who hadn't left her side. "It's the son we wanted." Then she asked no one in particular, "Isn't he beautiful?"

"He is indeed." Beau glanced at Savanah who was visibly moved and wondered if she was remembering another birth. She'd been alone, without his support and encouragement, and now he understood why she'd felt so abandoned.

He watched the new parents experience the miracle that was their newborn child and was filled with an old emotion he'd thought dead and buried for all time. Love for Savanah. He'd thought he'd never love again, but now it filled his heart to overflowing.

He was also filled with a profound regret that he hadn't been there to share in the joy of his own son's birth. He hadn't delivered that many babies in his short career, but each time had been touching and re-affirming.

"Well, young man," Savanah said as she took the now quiet baby from Beau. "Let's get spruced up for Mama while the doctor finishes up." She directed the overwhelmed new father to the kitchen for coffee while she washed, weighed and measured the baby.

Later, at Betsy's bedside, they all shared a glass of wine to toast the new arrival. "Six pounds, three ounces and eighteen inches long. Not bad for an early bloomer," commented Beau.

"A fine, healthy boy. He checked out in all departments," Savanah added. "Have you decided on a name yet?"

Shyly, Betsy looked up from the tiny bundle. "We're going to call him James Robert after Jimmy and my daddy. It'd mean a lot to the family."

Beau smiled. "That's a good, strong name and it will give him something to aspire to."

"But," Betsy hastened to add, "Jimmy and I've been talking, and we'd like to call him Beau."

"If you don't mind," her husband said with a quick look in Beau's direction.

"Mind? Why, I'd be honored."

"It seems only fitting after the way you took us in and all," the young man declared. "I don't know what we would've done without you and Savanah."

"It was my pleasure." Beau glanced at the tray Savanah had prepared for the hungry new mother. "Why don't we leave you alone now so you can get acquainted with Master Crawford?"

"Yes," Savanah agreed. "The ambulance will be here soon to take you and little Beau to the hospital. The nurses in the maternity ward will take good care of you, and after a few days of rest you can all go home."

Jim pumped Beau's hand vigorously. "Thanks again, Doc, for making arrangements for us and all. It was mighty good of you."

Beau was embarrassed that his outbreak of generosity was being noted. The young couple had been dismayed when he'd told them he'd called an ambulance and admitted Betsy and the baby to the hospital. They had no insurance and little money, but he'd told them not to worry—he'd taken care of everything.

He returned the handshake. "I don't knit, and it's too wet to go shopping, so I figured it was the least I could do to welcome our new arrival." His slender finger gently caressed the sleeping baby's downy-soft cheek.

"I don't know how we'll ever repay you," Betsy said with tears in her eyes.

"Just take good care of him, that's payment enough."

Savanah's heart nearly burst when Beau made the selfless gesture toward the penniless young couple. Later, after the little family left for the hospital, she mentioned it to him, but he'd dismissed it by saying, "Isn't that what Doc Ashburton would have done?"

"Yes."

"So, what makes you think Doc Beaulieu's any different?"

She rushed into his arms and they held each other, still exhilarated by the miracle they'd helped to happen.

After long moments he whispered, "Do you think we've just put in a hard day's night?"

"I think an appendectomy and a baby in the same day qualifies. The ambulance drivers joked that you've got them working overtime."

"I couldn't have done it without you," he said honestly.

"You did good, Doc. You'd better watch out, you're becoming indispensable around here."

He grinned. "The only person I want to be indispensable to is you."

She didn't answer because it was all too true already, and she feared he didn't mean it.

"I hope Doc has something stronger than peach brandy because we've earned a drink. Will you stay for a while?"

They stood together, his arm around her shoulders, hers around his waist, and watched the storm through the window. Strong wind lashed the trees in the yard and frequent jagged streaks of lightning were followed by earsplitting crashes of thunder.

She knew she wasn't going anywhere.

Chapter Eight

"Alone at last." He'd said it before as a joke, but this time he meant it. Beau smiled and handed Savanah a glass of wine. She seemed more relaxed than she had since he'd arrived in Harmony, but he was impatient. It was time to storm the doors of her heart, time to revoke the hands-off treaty she'd insisted on, once and for all.

If anyone had told him a few days ago that they'd be sitting together, sipping wine and discussing work, he wouldn't have believed it. Here they were, doing exactly that and he was failing miserably in the small-talk department. This wasn't exactly the way he wanted to spend an evening with Savanah.

He wanted to take her in his arms, and by word and deed of mouth convince her that he loved her—that he wanted and needed her. Kit was an added bonus, but not the only reason he wanted them to be a family.

"It's been a long day. You must be tired." Savanah tried to think of something funny that would make him laugh, something to dispel the tension between them. If she could put him in a lighter mood, maybe she could inch closer to him. She wished for the nerve that would allow her to fling herself into his arms and beg him to make the world disappear.

Tonight she'd watched him bring a child into the world and witnessed his compassion and capacity for love. What she'd seen had filled her with regret and guilt. Regret that she hadn't been brave enough to risk rejection nearly six years before, and guilt because she hadn't tried harder to tell him she was pregnant with his child.

So much time had passed that their differences had assumed an importance out of all proportion to reality. The problems of their relationship were like an open wound that had been neglected. It had become septic and could no longer be treated. Amputation, a clean break, was the only recourse.

"I'm going to look outside again." Beau ambled into the hall, not really caring about the weather but needing something to do.

The wind had picked up speed and swooshed inside when he opened the door. While the rain had slackened, the cold night air carried memories of winter. The tempest outside was abating, but Beau was more concerned about the emotional storm raging on in Doc's living room. Clouds of suspense and expectancy gathered there, just as thunderheads had gathered in the heavens. He'd promised Savanah not to take advantage of the chemistry between them, but that same chemistry was building in turbulence and threatened to erupt in a fury.

"I'm glad Pippy and Jasmine stayed over in Atlanta," he said as he reseated himself in the middle of the long sofa. "That wind would have made driving difficult. Do you miss Kit?"

"Yes, he's never spent a night away from me before." Beau had drawn attention to the fact that they were truly alone for the first time, and she'd drawn attention to the fact that he'd never spent a night *with* his son. She tensed.

"Tired, Savanah?"

"A little. It's a good kind of tired, though." He was so gentle, she thought, and kind and unexpectedly modest. His special brand of humor made her laugh, and his persistence was enough to make her scream. The nearness of his strong, lean body sent shivers of desire racing along every nerve path and as far as she could tell, he wasn't even trying.

Recently, she'd come to see another side of Gordon Beaulieu. Not only was he a talented and skilled physician, he was a wonderful human being. She wished things hadn't gone sour for them, that they had done things differently when it might have mattered. She'd always been taught to change the things she could and to accept those she could not. It was too late to change anything now, so all she could do was accept. She sighed thoughtfully and sipped her wine.

Beau didn't like the sound of that sigh. He refilled their glasses and said cheerfully, "Why don't I fix us a snack?"

Savanah groaned. "As I recall, you were never very handy in the kitchen. I haven't forgotten the last time you cooked something for us. I had to take you to the emergency room."

Beau set the glasses on the low table in front of the sofa and grinned mischievously. "I can't believe you'd bring that up. You have a cruel streak, you know that?"

Savanah widened her eyes innocently. "Me?"

"Yes, you. That's the thanks I get for being a romantic guy, for trying to prepare an erotic little open-hearth meal. I got the idea of eating in front of the fireplace from one of your women's magazines."

"But we didn't have a fireplace. Fondue wasn't meant to be cooked over an hibachi, and you could have burned down the whole apartment." Savanah lifted her chin in a defiant disclaimer, but their gazes locked, and she lost herself in the reflection of his twinkling eyes.

"It's the thought that counts," he said softly with a half grin. "Besides, with a hysterical wife at the wheel, I was in more jeopardy during the ride to the E.R." Beau leaned toward her.

He was so close all she'd have to do was move the slightest bit, and their shoulders would touch. "I was so worried. There was so much blood, and we were delayed by the fire department. I was practically frantic by the time..."

He patted her knee. "But it was only a scratch," he reminded.

Savanah swallowed. "Well, head wounds can be serious. I didn't mean to clobber you with that fire extinguisher. I was such a klutz."

"But a sweet klutz." Although they didn't have many, memories of being in love and happy together had kept Beau going. He wanted to pull her into his arms and talk about those joy-filled days, to share the warmth. Instead he laughed nervously and moved to the hearth. "Do you suppose it would be safe if I built a small fire?"

"Sure. That's a regulation fireplace, and I promise not to hit you with anything harder than a pillow." Thoughts of their marriage always brought bedroom furnishings to Savanah's mind. But then that's where they'd spent most of their time together. She felt the heat in her cheeks and knew at the rate she was going, it wouldn't be long before she blurted out that Doc's lumpy old couch made out into a bed.

She mentally chided herself and headed for the kitchen. "I'll get the food while you tend the fire. I'll see if I can find something that doesn't require toasting over open flames."

"Good luck. I've been eating at your house so often that I haven't done much shopping."

She opened the refrigerator. Soft drinks, beer, milk. That last had to be for Kit, but judging by its distinctive odor, he hadn't had any for a while. Grape jelly and marshmallow crème had never seemed appetizing to her. She'd given Betsy the last of the cheese and crackers, and there didn't appear to be much else.

She opened another cupboard and smiled. So this was where Doc stockpiled the products of Pippy and Jasmine's canning labors that they forced on him.

"How do you feel about pickled cauliflower?" she called to Beau.

"Ugh!" Beau scrunched up his nose. "What happened to good old bread and jelly?"

"Old is the operative word here. I don't know about you but I'm not into penicillin sandwiches."

"No." Beau thought a moment. "How about some raisin bran?"

"Stale cereal will go great with the clabbered milk."

"Never mind," came his answer.

"I can see you aren't an easy man to please."

She thought he said, "No. Just easy." But she couldn't be sure.

"How about Pippy's famous green tomato chutney? It won a blue ribbon at the county fair four years in a row." She waited for his response.

"I don't even know what that is."

"Peach conserve?" she tried again.

"What'll we do, lick it off the backs of our hands?" he yelled. "Are there any other kind of peaches?" he asked in a husky tone. "I'm really partial to sweet little Georgia peaches."

Only Beau could give sensual connotations to a discussion of food. Savanah peered at the fancy handwritten labels adorning each jar, reading them aloud and pausing after each for Beau's decision. "Peach butter? No... Spiced peaches? No... Brandied peaches?"

"That sounds promising. Let's try some of those."

She carried them into the living room, and Beau rubbed his hands together gleefully in boyish enthusiasm. The fire was burning brightly, but it was the only thing that was. He'd turned off all the lights.

She smiled as she handed him the jar. "Be careful with those. Jasmine has a pretty heavy hand when it comes to spirits."

"I will. Don't forget, I've already sampled the brandy." He removed the lid and sniffed appreciatively.

Savanah fell back on the couch. "Whoops, I forgot to bring in something to serve with."

Beau put a staying hand on her arm and dug in his pocket. "Surgeons and Boy Scouts are always prepared. We never go anywhere without our trusty pocketknives." He produced it triumphantly. "It may be primitive, but it's serviceable."

Savanah laughed as he wiped the blade and dipped it into the jar. He speared a peach half, then put the whole thing in his mouth. Juice trickled from one corner. "S'good," he mumbled inelegantly.

She stopped in midlaugh, her eyes glued to the sweet droplet that trembled on his bottom lip. The pain in her chest reminded her to breathe, and it was all she could do to resist the urge to capture it with her tongue, to experience the sweetness—and she wasn't talking peach juice.

Beau smiled, his eyes gleaming rakishly as he quartered a plump peach, fixed it on his knife and leaned toward her. "Want some?" he whispered.

Savanah's gaze held his, and her mouth opened to accept the offering. She scarcely noticed the trickle of juice that dribbled down her uplifted chin before it was replaced by his warm tongue, lapping it away. She almost choked before she remembered to chew and swallow.

Wordlessly, he handed her the knife and jar of sweet fruit. Lancing a dripping morsel, Savanah raised it to his waiting mouth. His lips closed over the knife and held her hypnotized as they slid recklessly off the sharp edge. His actions were almost as dangerous as the ache that was growing inside her, and she was helpless to do anything about it.

She couldn't stop herself from leaning into him, from allowing her hungry lips a sample of him.

"More," he whispered.

"I can't."

"I'm starving, Savanah."

"How can you trust me to feed you with this knife? My hands are shaking."

"Peaches won't satisfy me." He took the knife and jar from her nerveless fingers and set them on the table.

"That was wise. As clumsy as I am around you, it's a wonder I haven't scarred you for life."

"But you have," he said seriously, his gaze trapping hers. Beau took her hand and placed it over his heart. "You really did a number on me, you carved your name on this, and it's no good for anyone else. It can love only you."

Savanah wasn't sure who made the next move, the only certainty was that she was where she wanted to be. Back in Beau's arms, his lips devouring hers. Nothing else mattered. It was as if the moment were frozen in time. Nothing had passed before. Nothing would come after.

It was the most natural thing in the world when he pushed her gently to the floor. When his hands eased open her blouse. When he guided her arms around his neck. Bending low, he kissed the soft warm skin above her heart. His lips lingered there, and his warm breath sent little sparks of desire to the peaks, while his fingertips gently outlined the circles of her breasts.

Savanah tugged open his shirt and slipped her hands inside, her fingers tangling in the soft mat of hair on his chest. Beau took in a quick hard breath; wanting her was a pain inside him.

She caressed the bare flesh just above his hips, exulting in remembered pleasure. Had it really been nearly six years since they'd last loved? It seemed as if they'd never parted. Beau's muscles were hard and honed to athletic perfection, and she had a brief memory of him on the tennis court. He played as he did everything else, with a jackhammer intensity, a joy in doing and being. This perfect man was once more, at least for now, hers.

"I want to love you, Savanah," he said, rolling over her and kissing her eyes, nose and cheeks.

"I want you too, Beau," she whispered, curling her fingers in his hair to bring his lips back where they belonged, on hers.

He pulled back and looked into her eyes. "Savanah," he breathed, his voice thick and throaty. "I've needed you for so long. Just to hold you in my arms again feels wonderful."

Their lips met, his tongue outlined the opening of her mouth, and beyond. His hands slid over her ribs with deliberate slowness. She waited, suspended in time, breath caught in her throat, eager for the caress of his palms against her throbbing breasts.

His hands slid inside her blouse, cupping her breasts, and he kissed her again, his tongue probing, demanding, receiving all he asked for. He moaned and she answered in kind as they gently removed one another's clothing.

A light flared in Beau's dark eyes as he drank in the beauty of her naked body. He swallowed hard, struggling to control the primitive need arising in him.

She trembled and her body yearned for his. She was lost in love and desire, consumed by him and aware of nothing save his hunger and her own. A hunger too long denied.

Holding one another desperately, they sank once more to the floor, kissing in wild abandon, rediscovering one another's bodies with hands, lips and tongues. Shivers of pleasure seared bare skin. They breathed in jerky gasps until their minds and bodies exploded with pleasure.

"Savanah," Beau sighed as he collapsed beside her and wrapped her in his arms. Slowly rationality returned, and he became aware of their surroundings. He sat up languidly, stood and pulled her up with him, leading her upstairs to his bedroom.

"We can't..." she began, but he quieted her protests with his fingertips.

"Not yet, we'll talk later. Right now I need to hold you and be held, the way we used to."

"I need that, too."

They slipped into bed, finding joy in one another's arms. They were content for the moment not to worry about the future, to snuggle together and luxuriate in the happy afterglow of their lovemaking.

Later, after another, sweeter and much slower rediscovery, she felt his hold on her relax and knew he'd drifted off to sleep. She smiled, rubbing her face against his chest. He was right. There was nothing to say. Tomorrow would be another matter, but tonight they'd been beyond words. Still wearing a smile, she slept, too.

"Anybody home? Hey, Beau!" Doc Ashburton called from downstairs.

"Damn," Beau muttered when his benumbed mind finally registered the fact that they were no longer alone in the house. He scrambled out of bed and into as much of his clothing as he could find and took the stairs two at a time. When he reached the foyer he said, with more enthusiasm than he felt, "Why, Doc, what a pleasant surprise."

Up in Beau's room, Savanah dressed frantically, thankful they'd had the foresight to bring their discarded clothing upstairs with them. She buttoned her blouse and finger combed her hair. Not sure she could face Doc, but knowing it was now or never, she slowly descended. "Hi, Doc. You're home early."

"Well, hello, Savanah, my girl." Doc's eyes widened behind his glasses and his bristly gray mustache twitched. "Too early, from the looks of things."

"We can explain . . ." she began lamely.

"No need to. I came back for Kit's birthday. It is today, isn't it?"

"Yes." Savanah studied the pattern in Doc's worn foyer rug, and Doc mumbled something about not knowing who was the most surprised. She cringed.

Beau wasn't particularly uncomfortable. A man needn't feel ashamed for making love to his wife, but Savanah was clearly embarrassed by this unfortunate turn of events. "I'll explain everything, Doc. But first I'll walk Savanah home."

Doc shuffled to the door and held it open for her. "I'll listen to your explanations later. Right now, I'm walking Savanah home myself."

Beau ran his hand through his hair and started to protest, but Savanah intervened. "I'm ready when you are, Doc."

They talked about the storm as they crossed the street, and she asked Doc about his trip. It wasn't until they were seated in Pippy's kitchen, their hands cupping steaming mugs of tea, that they got to the heart of the matter.

"I'm sorry," Savanah blurted.

Doc peered at her over his bifocals. "Sorry?"

"I know what you must think of me," she said, her finger tracing the design of the linen tablecloth.

"Then you must know I think you're a damn fine woman, Savanah. I'm asking your permission to put in my two cents worth, and if you don't want to hear it, then don't listen."

Doc rubbed his grizzled cheeks, looked at her thoughtfully, then began. "I cleared your mouth so you could draw your first breath, and of all the children I've brought into the world, you've been most like my own. You're good to those two old ladies, and you're a devoted mother. Lord knows you got your hands full around here, and I've been concerned about you for a good spell, little missy. Far as I can tell, you never do have one iota of fun."

He looked up at the ceiling and squinted at the overhead light. "You may not like me buttin' into your business, but as one of the people who love you, I feel duty-bound to ask if you and Beau are planning to re-marry?"

"What?" she squeaked.

"You heard what I said, I didn't stutter. It's my ed-ucated guess that young man bunking at my place is your former husband and Kit's father. Tell an old fool he's right."

Savanah looked him in the eye and raised her chin a fraction. "Yes, Beau is Kit's father," she admitted.

"And did he shirk his responsibilities to you and the boy?"

Savanah shook her head. "He never knew about Kit. Not until he arrived here."

"Mmm-hmm." Doc nodded, then his face bright-ened. "Well, then, all you have to do is get married again."

"We're still married," Savanah said with a nervous laugh. "It seems that due to a failure on the part of a shade-tree lawyer, the marriage was never annulled as we'd thought."

"Good Lord," Doc exclaimed, slapping the table with both hands. "And I stumbled in and interrupted the happy reunion, huh?"

"Oh, Doc. It wasn't like that at all."

"Now, Savanah, I ain't blind. It's five in the morning. Beau came down putting on his clothes, and you were right behind him. Don't look now, gal, but your blouse is buttoned all wrong."

Savanah glanced down and realized her hasty job had indeed been faulty. "Oh, no."

"And I ain't too old to recognize that gleam in Beau's eyes when he looks at you. Why, anybody can plainly see he's crazy about you."

"Actually, he's crazy about his son."

"I'm mighty glad to hear that. What does Kit think about having a daddy sprung on him all of a sudden?"

"Kit worships him, but he doesn't know Beau's his father."

"Why not? What in the world have the two of you been doing the last two weeks?" he said. With a smile, he added, "No, no, don't answer that. Like I said, it's none of my business."

"Beau and I won't be getting back together, Doc. Ever."

Doc's mustache drooped. "You and Beau love each other," he insisted. "I knew there was some reason you never showed an interest in the young fellas around here. I didn't ask, but I suspected you were carrying a torch for somebody. Now that I've met him, I'm relieved to know he was worth it. He is worth it, isn't he?"

Savanah's eyes shone. "Oh, yes. He stepped in and almost filled your shoes," she said with a tender smile. "I'm very proud of the doctor and the man he's become." She proceeded to tell about the rash of medical emergencies and of Beau's grace under fire.

"He's a fine man. One worthy of your love," Doc told her when she was finished.

She sobered and some of the light faded from her eyes. "Beau loves his son, Doc. I just happen to be handy, part of the deal."

"Savanah, my girl, you're a hardheaded fool if you believe that. I knew there was strong stuff between you two the first night he arrived. I could feel the sparks leaping between you."

"There is something," she admitted. "But it wasn't enough to keep us together before, and it still isn't."

"Dang it, gal," he exclaimed. "Do you love him or not?"

"Yes, but—" she stopped and covered her face with her hands. "Love isn't always enough. We're too different to ever be happy together. We don't want the same things out of life."

"That sounds like a good excuse but what's your real reason?"

"I'm afraid of being hurt again," she said with a sob. She told him all about Beau's broken engagement to Christine and how it made her doubt the sincerity of his feelings for her now.

Doc patted her shoulder. "Let an old man give you a little advice. Love can hurt, but it can heal, too. A long-lasting love, one that can survive the test of time, doesn't come along every day. When it does you should grab hold of it, and hang on for dear life. Be thankful you were one of the lucky ones and rejoice in it. If you lose it, the memories of it will help you love again.''

Savanah looked at Doc and smiled. ''Isn't that a variation of the old 'Tis better to have loved and lost, then never to have loved at all' theme?''

Doc scratched his bald head. ''Now that you mention it, I reckon it is. But it has got to be old because it's good advice.''

''I don't know.'' Savanah laid her head on the table. ''I remember how I felt when I lost him the first time, I don't think I could bear to suffer like that again.'' She yawned. ''I'm too exhausted to worry about it. I haven't been getting much sleep lately.''

He patted her hand. ''Go to bed, Savanah. We'll talk again.''

At the door, she rushed into the old man's arms and cried. Doc was the surrogate father she'd always leaned on, the one whose advice she'd always trusted. He held her gently and, as though he knew it was what she needed, he let her cry, offering no meaningless words of comfort. She drew from his strength, and when she was cried out she pulled away and swiped at his shirtfront.

''I didn't mean to bawl all over you,'' she said with a small laugh.

''What the hell?'' he said, his own voice gruff with emotion, ''I won't rust.'' He gave her a reassuring pat and stepped out into the pinkening dawn.

Savanah watched until he'd entered the house across the street before closing and locking the door. She needed to lie down and think. Her chest ached as she trudged up the stairs to her bed and she wondered if the pain was her heart breaking.

"I hope you didn't say anything to upset her." Beau was pacing the floor when Doc came in.

"I don't think it was anything I've said that's got her in such a state." Doc padded into his book-lined study, indicating that Beau was to join him. He settled into an old chair that had long ago molded itself to the contours of his body and sighed in satisfaction. "The whiskey's in the third drawer of my desk, and there's paper cups in there too, if you don't like swigging it straight from the bottle."

Beau looked at him in surprise. "Whiskey? At this hour?"

"I don't know about you, young fella, but I need one for medicinal purposes."

Beau found the bottle and cups and placed them on the table beside Doc. "What did she say? What did you say to her?"

Doc poured two shots into the cups and handed one to Beau. "To young love," the old man toasted enthusiastically.

Beau couldn't refuse the toast, so they bumped cups and he took a sip. He coughed and his voice was raspy when he said, "I shouldn't drink to young love. That emotion is wasted in the hands of the immature. If Savanah and I had been a little older and a lot smarter when we met, things wouldn't have ended like they did. I'm sure of it."

"Sit down, boy, you're making me tired just watching you." Doc gestured to the ottoman and Beau sat.

"Did Savanah tell you we're still married?"

"Yes, as a matter of fact she did." Doc poured them a refill. "Shall we drink to your son?"

"To my son, Kit," Beau said proudly, and they drank again. "She named him Christopher after me. That's my middle name."

"I figured as much. Couldn't get her to name him Milton." Doc peered over his glasses and frowned. "She says you never knew about the boy until you came here, that she never told you." Doc rubbed his chin. "Don't that make you mad?"

Beau stared into his cup. "I admit I was angry at first, but she had tried to tell me." He explained about the letters. "I'm furious at my mother for keeping us apart, and I'll have to deal with her later. I'm beginning to understand how Savanah must have felt. I might have done the same thing in her place."

Doc shook his head. "I'm not sure I understand all this."

"Savanah and I met at a party—you know, eyes locking across a crowded room and all that? We never knew what hit us, it was as if we intoxicated one another. She wasn't the type to fool around, and I respected that. She was the finest thing that ever happened to me.

"We couldn't bear to be separated, even for a few hours. We didn't want to be around others, we were content just to be in the same room. I knew she'd never live with me without marriage, and I admired her values. I loved everything about her. One night we were ... um ..."

Doc laughed. "Hell, Beau, I'm old but I ain't dead yet. Spit it out, boy."

Beau laughed self-consciously. "Things were getting hot and heavy, and this time Savanah didn't want to stop. I threatened to lock her in the closet if she didn't calm down, and we laughed about that. We were always laughing." Beau smiled at the memories.

"Don't stop now." Doc leaned forward.

"Savanah told me she loved me and was tired of self-denial, said she'd only been saving herself for me anyway, and that she should discuss our views on birth control."

"And did you?"

"We never got around to it." Beau grinned sheepishly. "I had to do some fast talking to convince her that the sooner we got married the better. Savanah was concerned that Pippy and Jasmine would be disappointed by missing the hoopla and fuss of a big wedding, but neither of us had enough patience to wait several months for a planned event. The next thing we knew we were man and wife. She loved me then, and I think she loves me now."

"I think so, too."

"But she won't admit it. Not to me or herself. I don't think she trusts me completely, and trust is the biggest part of love. I realize now that trust comes with understanding, but we've spent the last six years trying to convince ourselves we didn't care for each other, and it will take a while to undo all the damage. I just have to convince her."

"She always was a stubborn little filly," Doc conceded. "What are your plans? I'm assuming, of course, you do have some."

"I'm taking her and Kit to Stone Mountain this weekend," he said. "But I don't know if it will do any good. Her mind seems to be made up."

"The opera's not over till the fat lady sings," Doc said. "Hang in there, boy, Savanah's worth fighting for."

"I know that, Doc."

"Too bad you couldn't get her to consent to a weekend for just the two of you."

"I've come a long way just to get her to agree to this much."

"She probably feels safer with the boy along," Doc suggested.

"Actually, I want us to be together, as a family. I want her to see what our life could be like if she'd let it."

"I knew you were a smart man the minute you opened your mouth." Doc winked. "Even if it was filled with a lot of Yankee mishmash. Savanah's a tough gal, but supposing you manage to wear her down, have you given any thought to what happens afterward? She's got ties here, you know."

"Yes, I realize that, and I've thought about it. Pippy and Jasmine say they can take care of themselves and I believe them, but I'm sure Savanah will want to be close by. I also wouldn't want to deprive the ladies of Kit and Savanah, they'd all miss each other terribly."

Doc nodded. "It sure is a problem."

"I'd miss them myself. I've grown very fond of Pippy and Jasmine."

"You should have seen 'em when they were young. The Jefferson gals always were a couple of real spark plugs. They turned their pappy's hair gray with their antics."

Beau said thoughtfully, "I've got an offer from a hospital in Atlanta. It isn't so far away, and maybe we can find a house on the outskirts. Or I could commute from a small town nearby. I'm willing to do anything to make Savanah happy."

Doc smiled. "I'm mighty pleased to hear you say that, son. I'm beginning to think things will work out just fine. I'll keep an eye on those two across the street."

"I'm happy to hear that, Doc. It'll ease Savanah's mind on that score." Beau's smile faded when he remembered there was a bigger obstacle in their path to happiness—a problem harder to solve than simple logistics. "Doc, we have to keep in mind that Savanah hasn't consented to anything yet."

"I have faith in you, Beau." Doc laughed.

Beau was glad to know that everyone who mattered to Savanah would be happy to see them get together. She'd hidden away from life long enough; it was time she left Harmony. He could only hope she'd be willing to leave with him and start a new life for the three of them elsewhere.

The weather had cleared, and the sky was crystal clear blue after being washed by the rain. Despite the storm the night before, Kit's birthday party was held

on a sunny Friday, which left no doubt that spring had
arrived. Judging by the noise level and cake con-
sumption, the party was a roaring success. The tiny
guests, which included the entire student body of
Smiley Face Playschool, would no doubt rate the event
one of the highlights of the season.

Beau conducted a raucous game of musical chairs
in the backyard and Aunt Jasmine, who had previously dismissed children's games as being "much too
rowdy," joined in. Pippy provided the music, her an-
cient concertina wheezing over the shouts and laughter of the children.

Not only had Kit gotten the fishing trip he'd asked
for—they had only caught three small perch between
them and had to go out to the Catfish Corral for a real
fish dinner—he also received a two-wheeled bike from
Beau. Now it was evening, and he had trouble settling
down to bed after such an exciting day. Savanah was
beginning to lose her patience. "Kit, you've had two
drinks of water in the last ten minutes. It's late."

"But..." Kit stopped midwhine when the door
opened and Beau poked his head into the room. "Hi,
Beau," he called, bouncing on the bed.

"Hello, sport." Beau looked at Savanah. "I was
hoping I could help tuck him in."

"Come on in," she said, smiling. She was inordi-
nately pleased to see him but not at all surprised. He
and Doc had stayed for dinner, and the whole group
had worked together to set the kitchen back to rights.
After Doc went home and Pippy and Jasmine had re-
tired, Kit brought out his new games. Beau and Sa-

vanah and their son had played each one, and it was now well past the child's normal bedtime.

Beau sat down on the bed, his knees touching Savanah's. "Aren't you sleepy, son?"

"Nope." Kit shook his head. "What are we gonna do now?"

"We may have to tie him in with the bedsheets," Beau said with a villainous leer.

Kit giggled. "Why don't you tell me a story," he suggested, plumping his pillow.

"Okay, lie down," Beau said and was surprised when the boy did so without argument. "Once upon a time, there was a little prince who wouldn't go to sleep. The king and queen had promised to take him to visit a wonderful kingdom."

"What kind of kingdom?" Kit was blinking, trying to stay awake.

Savanah looked down at their knees, hiding a smile.

"A magic kingdom filled with all the latest fun things to do and zillions of interesting things to see. Animals, too. The little prince could hardly wait to get there."

"What kind of animals?" Kit interrupted, then yawned.

Savanah coughed and looked away.

Beau shrugged and continued, his eyes widening like those of a mesmerist. "All kinds. But when morning came and it was time to depart, the little prince was too tired and cranky to make the long journey with the king and queen."

Savanah rolled her eyes to the ceiling, trying to keep a straight face.

"He pro'bly had to take a nap in the royal carriage, huh," Kit suggested.

"Alas," Beau intoned with mock sadness. "While it broke their hearts to do it, the king and queen had to leave the little prince behind with the royal baby-sitters and go on the journey alone."

Kit grinned. "Aw, Beau, that ain't a real story. You just made it all up."

"That's right," Beau agreed. "But it was a story. And you're going to sleep now, aren't you, sport?"

"Yeah, I don't wanna stay home with them royal baby-sitters. 'Specially if we go to the Atlanta Zoo. I wanna show you the telebishon set I bought for Willie B. back when his got stolen."

"You helped, Kit," his mother said. "You sent all the money in your piggy bank, when we read about it in the newspaper. That's called a donation."

"I can hardly wait to see the illustrious Willie B." Beau ruffled Kit's hair. "A black orangutan who loves television."

"Willie B. watches it all the time, doesn't he, Mommy?"

"That's what I hear," Savanah agreed.

"Can we take Beau to the zoo in Atlanta, Mommy? Can we?"

"I thought you wanted to go to the Wren's nest," she countered.

"We'll do both," Beau suggested. "If everyone gets to sleep very soon."

"Oh, boy, I'm almost asleep, already. You'll see." Kit's head fell back against the pillow, and he closed his eyes so tightly his nose was wrinkled by the effort.

Savanah and Beau tucked the covers around him, and she leaned over for her good-night kisses and hugs. "I love you," she said.

"Love ya', Mommy. Tomorrow's gonna be special, isn't it?" Kit asked Beau.

"Very special. The whole weekend will be filled with surprises." Beau glanced at Savanah meaningfully.

"We'll have fun, won't we, Beau?" Kit asked, covering his mouth and yawning tiredly.

"Yes, we will, son." Beau leaned over and kissed his soft cheek. "And if I have anything to say about it, we always will."

With his tiny arms, Kit reached up and grabbed Beau around his neck, hugging him. "Night, Beau. Love ya'."

Beau had to blink several times or he'd have disgraced himself right then and there. He took a deep breath as he shut the door behind them. Taking Savanah's hand in his, pulling her along in his wake, he guided her down the stairs and out on the front porch.

Outside, Savanah threw her arms around his waist and held him. Beau wrapped his around her shoulders, bringing her body close to his.

"Are you crying?" he whispered into her hair.

"Just a little," she said with a sniff. "Are you?"

"Just a little." Beau put his hands on her shoulders to put her away from him, but she locked her hands behind his back.

"No," she moaned. "Don't look at me, Beau. I need to be held in your arms. Just hold me."

He did so, fiercely, hugging her so hard, he was afraid he'd hurt her. Yet he couldn't bring himself to let go.

"I'm sorry," she mumbled against his shirt.

"It's not hardship, Savanah, I love holding you."

"You know what I mean." She burrowed into him. "I've cheated you, and I've cheated our son."

"Don't heap all the guilt on yourself. I could have come after you, and God knows I wanted to. Pride was the only thing preventing me from doing just that. You're not to blame, we were both wrong."

They held each other for a long time, saying nothing, each taking strength from the other. Then Savanah kissed him. It wasn't a kiss of passion, but the loving expression of all they'd shared, all they'd missed.

"I'd better go in," she said shyly, embarrassed that she'd initiated their closeness.

"I don't want to leave you," he replied.

"We'll be together all weekend," she reminded, pecking his cheek and backing away. She didn't bother to remind him they'd also have a built-in chaperon. "Good night, Beau."

"Good night, Savanah." For the first time since he'd set out to win her back, Beau was optimistic about the future.

He looked up in the sky and found what he thought was his old wishing star. As a child he'd wanted his parents to love one another again, so that he could have a real family. It was ironic that here he was, a grown man with a son of his own, wishing again. He'd changed roles, and now he was the father instead of the son. He was supposed to be grown-up, but he still felt a childlike faith when he looked at that wish-it-real star. He stood there a full minute, a dream in his heart, his gaze on a star.

Chapter Nine

A five-year-old boy in a theme park is easily distracted, and Kit soon proved to be a total washout as a chaperon. Beau was skilled at diverting the boy's attention and made the most of every opportunity to touch Savanah in some way. His ploys, ranging from snitching kisses when Kit wasn't looking, to tugging her hair affectionately when he was, were calculated to destroy her tenuous self-control and sabotage her own concentration on the sights and sounds of Stone Mountain.

The morning was still crisp when they rode Swiss-made cable cars on a breathtaking journey past the magnificent Confederate Memorial carving, the world's largest work of sculptural art, to the top of the granite mountain. Beau and Savanah were wedged on a bench seat with Kit squeezed between them.

"There's an empty seat, I'll move." She started to rise, but Beau reached out a staying hand, and her gaze was drawn to his long fingers spread possessively on her jeans-clad knee.

"Sit on my lap, son," he said to Kit. "We're squeezing Mommy like Pippy's concertina." Beau winked at Savanah.

"You're silly, Beau." Kit giggled and clambered up on his lap.

Beau's attention was claimed by the passing sights, and he seemed totally unaware of the warmth of his left arm where it lay along her leg, his fingers drawing lazy designs on her knee. His other arm hugged Kit's small shoulders, and the paternal gesture was equally unconscious on his part. But Savanah was aware of it. She was sensitive to the crisp, assertive scent of his after-shave. To the contrasting textures of his new-stiff jeans and his buffalo-plaid flannel shirt, which was as soft as a sigh.

She was becoming attuned to the cadence of his Bostonian speech, and it no longer seemed harsh to her. Like everything else about him it was—just Beau. She was growing accustomed to the acceleration of her heartbeat when he was near, to the tautness of her nerves that were in a constant state of excitement. Maybe he was oblivious to the sensory havoc he created, but she wasn't.

Beau's hands had never seemed so full before. Beneath one palm was the perfect woman, the one he wanted to spend the rest of his life with. The other caressed the small shoulders of their son. He imagined he could feel the energy, the love, flowing between the three of them, like electricity in an unbroken circuit. They formed a unit so perfect that Beau was suddenly gripped with another new emotion, and his heart swelled in his chest. Family pride was a fearsome thing. He'd never really felt a part of a family before, and he couldn't remember feeling as happy as he did now.

Later at the Trader's Camp, a lively petting zoo with tame deer, goats, rabbits and baby bison, located in a section of the wildlife trails, Beau and Savanah watched Kit pet every creature he could get close to. They bought some of the animals' special feed, and he made friends with a small African goat whose determination in sniffing out the goodies in Kit's pockets made the child squeal with delight. Beau thought he'd never heard a sound as beautiful as that of the mingled laughter of his wife and child.

When they took a walk through Section II of the wilderness area, Beau had to reassure Kit that the carnivores—mountain lions, river otters and wolves—living inside spacious natural enclosures were no threat to them. Just the same, Kit insisted on walking between his parents, clutching both their hands.

They toured the fascinating Antebellum Plantation where nineteen authentically furnished buildings had been carefully moved from the original site of construction and reassembled to recapture the atmosphere and flavor of the Old South. Beau was particularly intrigued by that long-lost way of life and consulted the guidebook for more information. Savanah was glad she'd seen it all before, because Beau was so compelling she couldn't keep her eyes off him.

The role he'd adopted seemed unnaturally natural for a man who'd been a bachelor up until a few weeks ago. He was the model of a loving father and attentive husband and had assumed his place as the dominant male in charge of the expedition. It wasn't difficult for her to picture him at the head of his own table, commanding the attention and respect of those gathered around it.

She shook her head to clear it of the image and watched him lift Kit to his shoulders so the child wouldn't miss any of the intriguing sights. He was clearly basking in their son's unqualified adoration.

Savanah tried not to worry about anything but the moment. Here and now was all that was important. She was too busy saving memories for later to dwell on the decisions she would soon have to make. Like Scarlett O'Hara, whose lifestyle they seemed immersed in at the moment, she would think about it tomorrow. She didn't want her warring emotions to spoil her enjoyment of the day and banished them from her mind.

Their cursory look-see of the Antique-Auto-and-Music Museum was hurried because Kit was too hungry to wait any longer for lunch. Afterward they took an old-fashioned steam-locomotive ride around the five-mile base of the world's largest granite monolith that gave the park its name.

Kit asked a million questions, which Beau patiently answered. Savanah couldn't guess how he came by all his information, but it was clear that he'd done his homework. Of course, Kit would have believed him if he'd said he had personally arranged for the earth to create the massive mountain for their enjoyment. She felt that way herself.

They boarded the riverboat, appropriately named the Scarlett O'Hara, for a scenic cruise around Stone Mountain Lake, which covered more than three hundred and sixty acres. Beau guided Savanah and Kit through the crowd to a vantage place at the rail, and placed his arm around her shoulders. He hadn't been able to keep his hands off her all day and enjoyed the closeness they'd shared.

They were like many other young parents, very much in love, on an outing with their child. He could pretend there was no rift between them, no talk of divorce and visitation. He couldn't help noticing, however, that while she'd allowed overtures on his part, she had not initiated any on her own.

Nothing had been resolved between them, except in his own heart and mind. He wondered if they might have talked things out, once and for all, if Doc hadn't come home when he had.

Now that Doc was back, he had no excuse for staying on in Harmony. Despite his fragile plans, he would soon have to leave if Savanah didn't make up her mind. He'd done everything he could to convince her of his love and would insist she make a decision, hopefully before the night was out.

He'd noticed the fear and doubt in her eyes today. She was nervous and reserved. He didn't know what more he could do or say to gain her trust. All he knew was that he loved her. He'd loved her before and he'd never stopped.

Despite her wariness, he felt she must surely share some of his feelings, or she never would have allowed things to go so far the night of the storm. She had responded to his lovemaking fiercely, aggressively. They'd always been able to excite one another to grand passion, but last night when they'd tucked Kit into bed, they'd attained a sense of comfort and peace that was a new element in their relationship.

It was sadly ironic, he mused, that the child they both loved, the child who should have brought and kept them together, was in fact an obstacle in convincing her of his love. He squeezed Kit's hand and smiled back when the trusting face looked up questioningly.

Savanah watched the sun play over the rippling water. The bright spring day gave no indication that there had been a storm only two nights before. The storm was inside her now. Beau's nearness and attentiveness were playing havoc with her heart and head. When he'd put his arm around her as the boat pulled out, she'd been tempted to fling hers around his neck and beg him to stay with her forever. She never wanted to be without his touch again.

She was astounded by her response to him. That stormy night, his body had promised and fulfilled her with unspoken delights, but last night he'd gently eased her heartache. Things had seemed possible that night, but sunshine had brought with it the shadows of doubt.

Beau loved Kit and the feeling was mutual. She couldn't deny that, and yet she couldn't believe his declaration of love for her. Several times today she'd caught him looking at her with a wistful expression on his face. It was the same one he wore when he looked at Kit.

Was it possible that he really loved her? Or were his feelings for her tied up so inexplicably with his feelings for their child that he didn't really know the difference? He'd admitted to convincing himself he loved Christine when the feelings weren't there, so it was possible he'd deluded himself again. Maybe she could have believed him if there weren't a history of pain between them.

Doc's return meant she could no longer afford the luxury of indecision. She would be forced to face the issue of divorce soon, but she didn't know what to think, and she certainly didn't know what to do.

"It's lovely isn't it?" she asked when she felt his gaze.

"Yes," he agreed, without taking his eyes off her. He leaned toward her, allowing only their shoulders to touch. Then the pressure of his fingers, which covered hers on the rail, increased. He brought the back of her hand against his chest and held it there.

Savanah could feel the uneven, heavy beat of his heart. His eyes closed slowly as his lips lowered to hers. The kiss was a gentle massage, full of unspoken yearning. Under her hand, his pounding heart went wild.

He drew away too soon. Resting his forehead briefly against hers, he clasped her hand in both of his and looked out over the shimmering water once more.

"Will you have dinner with me tonight?" he asked. "Maybe we could go dancing later."

"What about Kit?" she asked, her eyes lingering over his profile.

Beau's slow smile began in his eyes. "We can order him dinner from room service and use the hotel sitter service. I've already checked into it, and they have excellent credentials."

"Sounds like you have it all worked out."

"I told you I believe in being prepared. Besides, he'll be so exhausted he'll probably fall asleep in his plate."

"I think you're right." She wanted to be with Beau; they had so much to discuss. "Sure, it sounds like fun."

"Are you done kissin' yet?" Kit said impatiently. "Heck, you missed the best part, the ride's all over."

"That *was* the best part, son," Beau said with a laugh as he hoisted Kit up on his shoulders and took Savanah by the hand. "The ride is just beginning."

They managed to take in all the other sights without dropping from the tourist's occupational hazard—too much fun. After seeing to Kit's bath and dinner, Savanah tucked him into bed and waited for the sitter to arrive. When she was sure the middle-aged woman was competent, she knocked on Beau's connecting door and they told Kit good-night together.

Once seated in the restaurant, Beau had trouble taking his eyes from her and the outfit she wore. It wasn't just the dress or the fact that it was a becoming shade of pink, or that the skirt was very full and swirled lovingly around her shapely legs. It was strapless and seemed to defy gravity, making Beau doubt its ability to stay up on its own. After reflecting on that, he decided that he rather liked that aspect of her outfit best.

She felt his eyes on her, and one hand went involuntarily to her chest to make sure that everything was covered that should be. It was the same hand he'd held against his heart when he'd kissed her on the boat earlier, and it seemed to Savanah that it still tingled as she put it back in her lap.

During dinner they talked companionably about the day's events, and Kit's reaction to the things he'd seen. It soon became obvious to Beau that Savanah was making an extra effort not to give him an opening in which to bring up their future. He knew they would have time for that later and let her keep the conversational ball rolling.

While they waited for the check, they discussed places they might go for dancing. "Want to go to the Limelight?" he asked.

"I've never been there. They used to have a see-through dance floor, didn't they? With tigers underneath?"

"They did at one time, but now it's the place where most of the big-time artists appear when they're in Atlanta. Shall we try it? Or we could go to Harrison's or Elan's."

In the end they didn't go to any of those, choosing instead an obscure place with a piano bar. They sat on tall stools, listening to mellow tunes, sipping spindly glasses of Chablis. When the pianist eased into the first stains of a slow song, he guided her onto the tiny dance floor.

With her arms around him, her legs brushing against his, she followed his lead. He danced her into a corner where they only pretended to keep up with the music, studying one another's faces in the dim light.

"Do you know your eyes have a definite sparkle, even in the dark?" Beau linked his hands at the small of her back, bringing her lips suggestively closer.

She shook her head, then noticed a tiny scar at the corner of his mouth. Her fingertip moved to whisper across it. "How did you get this?"

"I believe that happened the first time I attempted to slide down a banister."

Savanah smiled. "Banister sliding doesn't seem to be your strong suit."

Beau laughed. "Oh, I don't know. You can run into some pretty interesting people that way."

One torchy love song faded into the next as they swayed against each other, moving languidly, her hands on his shoulders, his on her hips. They talked about anything and everything, sharing memories they'd thought forgotten.

Soon Savanah was relating stories about Kit's first years. Beau laughed or smiled, and she loved his expression and the way he eagerly asked more questions. He was crazy about his son and anxious to catch up on the everyday things he'd missed.

The magic cocoon they shared didn't begin to dissolve until they returned to the inn. Beau paid the sitter while Savanah made sure Kit was still asleep.

"Let's go in my room," he said softly. "We really need to talk. We'll leave the door ajar in case he wakes up." They walked into the other room. He took her hands in his as they sat knee to knee on the side of the bed. "Savanah, have you changed your mind about the divorce?" he asked without preamble.

She sighed, knowing that the question had been filling up his thoughts all evening as it had hers. "Please, Beau, don't start. I'll let you see Kit as often as you like, take him wherever you want. Isn't that enough for you?"

"No, dammit! It isn't." He slapped his knees. "I've missed enough. I've missed the anticipation of becoming a father and of seeing my son come into the world. I wasn't there to hold his hand when he took his first steps, to comfort him when he cried in the night. I didn't hear his first words or see his first tooth. I've never heard my son call me daddy." He stopped, unable to continue.

Beau's words opened a floodgate of emotions and unchecked tears streamed down her cheeks. He was right, all those things were irrevocably lost to him. "I'm sorry," she managed at last.

"Hell," he swore emphatically. "I'm not blaming you, I'm just trying to tell you how I feel."

"I know," she said softly. "I know."

"Then try to understand what I'm going to say. I don't want to miss another day, I want to spend every moment I can with him. I want to be the one to teach him to ride that new bicycle. I want to be there when he learns to drive a car, has his first date. I want us to be a family. I want him to know that I'm his father."

His words tore at her heart. Those were the very things she wanted too, but not this way. She wanted Beau to love her in spite of the fact that she was Kit's mother, not because of it. Beau had a right to claim his son, and Kit had the right to know his father. But she selfishly wanted to be a part of it, and hated herself for standing between them. "We don't have to stay married for him to know that. We'll tell him."

"I love you, Savanah," he ground out. "I want the three of us to live happily ever after. I want to have more children, and I want you to be their mother and me to be their father. I want us to spend the rest of our lives together." He took a deep breath and gathered his courage. Turning to her and taking her hands in his again, he asked softly, "Don't you feel anything for me at all?"

What she felt for him threatened to engulf her like a tidal wave. Love, passion, desire, all the things she'd tried to deny and couldn't. She couldn't admit to them, she couldn't even speak.

He brought one of her hands to his lips, placing a warm wet kiss in its center, then placed it over his heart. "Do you feel that?"

Savanah only nodded, and he lifted her other hand, cupping it over her own heart. "Even our hearts beat in perfect harmony," Beau said seductively. "Can you deny it?"

"No," she whispered. She was tired of denying. Another tear rolled down her cheek. "Please don't say tender things to me, you're trying to tempt me and it isn't fair."

Beau caught the salty drop with the tip of his tongue. "When I do this," his lips gently sucked her bottom lip, "Your pulses go crazy and so do mine."

"If I touch you here," he said, moving his hand to her breast, his thumb drawing lazy little circles that made her stomach ache with desire. "Your breast swells to fit exactly into the palm of my hand."

Savanah pushed away from him. "Stop it, Beau! We both know we're sexually attracted. We've had this talk before, sex isn't enough to make a marriage work."

Beau stared at her. "I'd certainly hate to be in a marriage without it. Maybe it didn't work out before, if you'd just give it a chance, we could make it turn out right this time."

Saying, even wanting something, didn't make it true despite his wish-it-real philosophy. She made an unplanned offer. "I'll give you joint custody. You don't have to take me to get Kit."

"If we can't be a family, I don't think I want custody at all." When Savanah's eyes grew wide in surprise, he hastened to add, "You've never been sent from one household to another, and you can't imagine what that's like."

Beau stood up and began to pace as he talked. "In the very beginning I felt as if I had no home at all. I didn't *really* belong anywhere. I was always on the outside, like a visitor who was only there on sufferance. One wrong move and I was out."

"But you and I wouldn't do that to Kit," Savanah argued.

"And my parents didn't really do that to me. I'm only trying to show you how I felt as a child. I was either living in my mother's house or my father's, but I had no place I could call home. If I told my mother I'd left a favorite toy at home, she'd look hurt because I'd called Dad's house 'home.' I knew I'd caused her pain, and it gave me a frightening sense of power.

"It was the same with my father. I was a perpetual visitor. After a time I learned to say mommy's house or daddy's house to differentiate between them, and once those words were spoken the feeling of not having a home of my own became real. For fifteen years I lived out of a suitcase. I couldn't go skiing with my father at Christmastime because it was my mother's year to 'have me.' When I was really small I agonized that Santa wouldn't know where to find me. He didn't know my schedule and might get mixed up. I worried that there wouldn't be any presents under the tree for me."

Savanah slumped. "It must have been hell."

"Poor little rich kid," Beau said derisively. "The best is yet to come. When I got older I realized there was a war going on, and I was the booty. All I had to do was tell Dad that Mother wouldn't allow me to ride a motorcycle and...bingo! I was the proud owner of the biggest, fastest motorcycle money could buy.

"Then I'd tell Mother Dad had given me a motorcycle, and before I could get the details out of my mouth, I'd have something else, more expensive. It was a game without winners."

Savanah looked up. "I don't think the situation is quite the same. I think parents who are unsure of their children's love use material generosity to convince themselves. Kit knows we love him, and that would never happen."

"Maybe not, but I wouldn't want to take that chance." Beau sighed. "As a child, I used to wish that some magic would bring my parents back together. That we'd be a family again. That they would stop fighting over me like two dogs with one bone. I don't want my son to go through that."

"Beau, I wish things were different."

"So do I, Savanah. Because I love you."

"If only I could believe that."

"I've done everything I know to convince you, to prove it to you, but I've failed." Beau took a deep breath. "I thought love would be enough, but it doesn't work without trust. Deep down, I'm not sure I trust you yet, either. I'm not sure I know you any more. But the difference is, I'm willing to risk it again."

Was he really? She had to wonder. He was safe in making such grandiose statements because he knew she couldn't take that risk. She wanted to. But she couldn't.

"I love Kit, and as much as I'd like to be a part of his life, I've decided we shouldn't tell him I'm his father." He turned to the window with unseeing eyes.

"What are you saying?" Behind him, she raised her hand to touch his arm, then let it fall to her side.

"I love you, but I couldn't bear to live on the edge of your life. I've told you how hard it could be on Kit, but there's another aspect that can't be ignored. A permanent link with Kit would mean a permanent pain for me, because eventually you'll find happiness with another man and I'd have to witness it. Through Kit

I'd know whether you were happy or sad, and both would be equally devastating.

"I've told you how I feel about joint custody. You don't want to be my wife, so I won't muddle up Kit's life with a long-distance father." He turned to her sadly. "It's best for all of us."

"Beau, you're making a decision based on emotion that would be better done with logic. You need time to think this over."

"I've thought about nothing else for the past two weeks. I told myself you cared for me once, and that you could care for me again. As hard as it is for me to accept, I understand that you don't love me enough to trust me, to live with me."

"Beau, it isn't that . . ."

"Don't explain," he said with a sad smile. "I don't think I could stand logic right now. I'll have my attorney draw up the necessary papers relinquishing my paternal rights. I know you'll feel safer with those in your possession." Beau crossed to the connecting door and opened it, waiting for her to leave.

There was no point in telling her about the Atlanta offer now. He wouldn't be taking it. That was a wish that would never come true.

"Beau, I . . ."

"You'll have to seek the divorce on your own. It would seem hypocritical of me to initiate proceedings feeling the way I do. But I won't give you any trouble. Anything you want, you can have." He'd declared his love for her, and she'd flung it back in his face. There was nothing left to say.

Savanah couldn't bring herself to walk through the door. Her back remained straight and stiff, but her spirit was in chaos. "You're making a totally unnecessary sacrifice. It's a mistake to give up Kit," she said, her voice thick and unsteady as she forced herself to take the final steps that would take her out of his life forever. "He'll be badly hurt."

"He's young. Children his age have a short memory, and in a year or so he won't even remember me. There will be a new hero in his life. Just make sure it's someone worthy of his admiration."

"Beau, I don't want you to do this."

"The disappointment and loss Kit will feel when I leave are nothing compared to what he would suffer if he had to divide his love between us. It really is the only thing I can do and live with myself. Now go, there's nothing left to discuss."

When she would have walked past him, he grabbed her. What the hell, he was damned if he did and damned if he didn't. Grasping her upper arms, he turned her body to his, pressing her against him.

The moment their mouths met, the anger and hurt were defeated by something much stronger, and he kissed her relentlessly. When at last he lifted his head, her lips were red and swollen, her eyes half-closed and limpid, her body heated and ready. Her breasts rose and fell with every breath, swelling above the neckline of her dress.

His head lowered to place a brushing caress on the bare skin above the strapless bodice before he drew away and backed off.

"Why did you do that?" she breathed.

"Because it's the last one I'll ever get, and I wanted it to be something to remember."

"Then you do understand?"

"No. I don't understand. I'm simply giving up."

Chapter Ten

"What's Beau up to?" Jasmine peered out the parlor window where she'd undertaken sentry duty. "Why, he's toting bags out to his car!" she gasped, dropping the lace curtain and marching across the room. She ground to a halt in front of Savanah, who was rocking industriously and blowing her nose. "*Why* is Beau toting bags out to his car?"

"I suppose he's going back to Boston," she sniffed. "He only came to visit. We all knew he wasn't staying forever."

"I declare! You really are the most obtuse girl, Savanah." Jasmine waved her hanky and flitted to the parlor door. "Sister, Sister! You better come quick."

Pippy rushed into the room, drying her hands on her apron. "What's all the ruckus about, Jasmine?"

"Mercy me, you're not gonna believe this." Jasmine fanned her face and sank down on the settee.

"Will you just spit it out, Sister, I've got baking to do."

"Baking? How can you think about muffins and popovers at a time like this?"

"A time like *what*, Jasmine? Whatever has put you in such a tizzy?"

"He's leavin'! Just like that." Jasmine snapped her fingers and the sound was audible over Savanah's sniffling and the clock's persistent ticking. "And worse of all, she's not doin' a thing to stop him."

Pippy bustled over to the window and squinted out. "Landsakes, Savanah, he is. When's he coming back?"

"Probably never," Savanah said sadly and promptly burst into tears. She'd been crying on and off ever since they'd gotten home a few hours ago. They'd make a quick tour of the zoo, just as Beau had promised Kit, but the closeness and fun they'd shared at Stone Mountain were gone. She'd waited for the right moment to approach him, to make some kind of amends, but it never came. He'd been unusually silent and brooding, speaking only when necessary and not once looking her in the eyes.

Savanah understood that he was trying to distance himself from them, to untangle his life from theirs. His sadness was enough to make her weep, it was as though his son were already lost to him and he had begun mourning.

Even Kit had sensed the change in their relationship and was ill-tempered and petulant. It was a relief for everyone when they decided to forego the Wren's Nest and finally started home. Kit had fallen asleep, and Beau had driven in stony silence, giving the road all his attention.

There was nothing left for Savanah to do but stare out the windows and think. She hadn't slept the night before; the state she'd been in was not conducive to relaxation. She'd thought about all Beau had said, vacillating between the desire to capitulate and resentment at the position he'd placed her in.

She felt guilty and sad and sorry and most of all, lonely. Several times on the brief drive home, she'd started to tell him she'd changed her mind, but he'd seemed so remote that the words were never spoken.

"I'll be right back," Pippy said, rushing out to the kitchen.

"All gone," Jasmine bemoaned as she paced, wringing her hands. "All our lovely plans. Gone."

"What plans?" Savanah asked, having regained a semblance of composure.

"Just all of them, that's what." Jasmine toyed with the bric-a-brac on a side table. "I can't tell," she said fretfully. "I swore I wouldn't."

"Tell what, Aunt Jasmine?"

She sighed. "Nothing, nothing at all." She returned to her vigil at the window. "Oh, no, he and Doc are on the porch now," she reported.

Pippy came back in time to hear the latest account and sat down across from her granddaughter. "It's true-confession time, Savanah. Why did Beau come here? And I want the truth."

Savanah hugged herself and rocked furiously.

Jasmine sat down beside Pippy. "We don't have much time, dear, so please be honest. Honesty is always the best policy, you know. Remember the time you..."

"Galloping goobers, Jasmine!" Pippy interrupted. "Let the girl talk."

The two little ladies waited expectantly, and she couldn't bear their scrutiny. She was reminded of her childhood, and the times she'd had to confess some small infraction for their absolution. Things were bad enough without being made to feel like a naughty child. She stood up. "I'd better see about Kit, he must be getting hungry."

"Kit's playing outside." Pippy took Savanah's hand and made room for her between them. "While I was in the kitchen I made him one of those disgusting sandwiches he loves so much. He's in fine shape, so sit down and come clean with us."

"I don't know where to start," she said lamely.

"Why not start with what went wrong at Stone Mountain. We thought you and Beau were ... well ... that things were... you know," Jasmine said with what was meant to be a suggestive wink.

"I don't know where you got that idea."

"Probably the same place everyone else did," Pippy remarked dryly, "from Beau and from you."

"What's that supposed to mean?" Savanah was indignant.

"We're wasting valuable time, pussyfooting around this. We already know *who* Beau is," Jasmine said with exasperation. A car roared off down the street, and she jumped off the sofa and hurried to the window. "It wasn't him," she said with relief. "He's still talking to Doc."

"Good," Pippy replied. "Savanah, we know Beau is Kit's father and your former husband. What we don't know is why you two got the marriage annulled in the first place."

Savanah sighed. "Actually we didn't."

"What!" they cried in unison.

Savanah owed them an explanation and gave all the details the two ladies demanded.

"That puts a whole new light on things, don't it, Sister?" Jasmine asked from her lookout post. Without waiting for an answer she updated the action across the way. "He and Doc have gone round to the backyard."

"Savanah," Pippy said, taking her hands in hers. "Beau loves you and he told you so. How can you let him drive right out of your life?"

"I don't know how to stop him."

"I'm a tired old lady," Pippy complained. "You'll have to explain that one."

"When Beau first came, there was no talk of love and staying together. He made it clear that while he was interested in exploring the...um...physical aspect of our relationship, he wasn't promising forever. Then when I told him about Kit, everything changed. Suddenly, he started talking family, and I was sure his offer was no more than a noble gesture.

"I wanted to believe it was more, but I couldn't trust his feelings for me any more than he could trust his own." Remembering his reluctant offer to step out of Kit's life forever, she went on, "Something he said at

Stone Mountain convinced me of his sincerity, but like a fool, I didn't realize it then. When I did it was too late.''

Pippy released a heartfelt sigh and fell back against the sofa cushions. "All these years apart haven't taught you a thing, has it?''

Savanah's eyes misted again. "I guess it just wasn't meant to be.''

"Does that mean we won't get to have the weddin' in the gazebo after all?" Jasmine wailed.

Pippy leaped to her feet. "This ain't the time to be worryin' about weddings and such. Time's awasting. We've got to do something.''

"There's nothing to do. Even if I do tell him how much I love him, he'd still have to leave.''

Pippy snorted. "Now that's what our pappy used to call 'pure-dee sheep-dip.' There isn't a reason in the world you three can't be together.''

"And where will we be together at?" Savanah asked. "He can't do what he wants to do here, be what he was meant to be. And I don't want to live in Boston.''

Jasmine turned from her window-gazing. "Now that really is sheep-dip. If you love him, it don't matter where you live.''

"Besides, Miss Smarty," said Pippy, "You don't know everything. Accordin' to Doc, Beau has a right temptin' offer from a hospital over in Atlanta. All you gotta do is say the word.''

At first Savanah couldn't believe her ears. He had a job offer in Atlanta? Why hadn't he told her? Why hadn't he used such leverage to influence her decision? With dawning awareness, she understood. Starting over didn't mean her moving to Boston or Beau staying in Harmony. It meant making a home for themselves in a place they'd known happiness before.

Wisely, he'd left it up to her to sever the ties that bound her to the bitter past. Savanah's heart at last accepted that theirs did not have to be a no-win proposition for either of them. But how to tell Beau? "If I only knew how."

Jasmine waved her hanky. "You want to lose him again? Get yourself out there and stop him."

"Hush up, Sister." Pippy put her arm around Savanah. "All that matters is you love each other. The where and the how don't amount to a hill of beans. It doesn't have to end like this."

"But it's too late," she cried.

"It's never too late," Pippy disagreed.

"When I tried to gather the courage to tell him I'd reconsidered, he was so unapproachable. What if he doesn't want me now?"

"Lordamercy," Jasmine screeched from the window. "Beau and Doc are shaking hands by the car. You'd better hightail it out there right now."

"He's not going anywhere, Doc promised to stall him," Pippy said smugly.

Savanah raised her head. "What can I do? How can I be sure he'll want to hear what I have to say?"

"Well, you can't sit there bawling the rest of your life," cried Jasmine. "Beau is Kit's daddy and you love him. You can't just sit idly by and let him drive away forever."

"Savanah, I'm surprised at you," Pippy scolded. "Nothing about love is ever certain. It's a gamble, just like life, but you have to try. There's winners and there's losers. Which one are you going to be?"

"Why's Mommy crying?" Kit came through the parlor door and sat down beside Savanah.

She hugged him tight. "It's okay, baby, Mommy's just sad." She kissed the top of his head.

"Oh," Kit said sagely. "'Cause you love my daddy and you're fixing to sit idly by and let him drive away forever?"

"Land-o-goshen!" Jasmine exclaimed. "That boy's got ears like a hawk."

Pippy snorted. "Everybody knows hawks don't have ears. They're famous for their good eyesight, you old fool."

"It's their hearing," Jasmine insisted.

"Eyes," Pippy intoned.

The verbal battle raged around them, but Savanah was more concerned about Kit. She hadn't wanted him to find out like this. In fact, he wasn't supposed to find out at all. She searched his face for a sign of anxiety, but all she saw was confusion. "Kit, how do you feel about all this? What do you think about Beau being your daddy?"

"I think it's neat," he said brightly. "I'm real glad 'cause I already love Beau and he loves me. We been buddies a long time now, but lately I've been wishin' and wishin' for him to be my daddy and now he is," he said with a triumphant smile. Then with adult seriousness he whispered, "I made it come true by wishing for it. I knew I could do it."

Like father, like son. Savanah sobbed again, but this time it was with joy.

"You're not gonna let Daddy leave us, are you, Mommy?" Kit asked in a small voice. "He don't want to."

Savanah hugged her son again. With a child's faith, Kit had believed in something that she had doubted and denied. She had stubbornly refused the love that had been there all along. Love that had been offered with a hope for their future as wistful as Kit's.

The arguing stopped and Pippy and Jasmine's ears perked in their direction. Jasmine glanced out the window and threw up her hands. "That's it, he's getting in the car."

"Here's what I want you to do," Savanah said, whispering in Kit's ear. "Have you got it?"

Kit nodded vigorously. "I got it."

"He's starting up the engine," Jasmine wailed.

Savanah grabbed Kit's hand, and they dashed out the front door and down the walk just as Beau backed out of the driveway across the street. "Hurry, Kit, before he gets away."

Kit opened the gate just as Beau shifted into drive and accelerated.

Beau had slipped on his mirrored sunglasses because he didn't want to advertise his emotional state to the whole world. Driving away from Savanah and Kit was the hardest thing he'd ever done, and he wasn't sure he'd ever get over it. He'd originally planned to stop and say goodbye but had decided against torturing himself in such a fashion. Savanah had made her position perfectly clear, and he couldn't bear the thought of a drawn-out farewell. It was best to just go.

"Daddy! Daddy!" Kit raced down the street behind the red car, his small legs tangling beneath him. "Daddy, please wait! We need you."

Beau couldn't resist one backward glance, and when he saw the small figure standing forlornly in the middle of the street, he slammed on his brakes, killed the engine and jumped out, leaving the car in the street with the door open. With long strides he walked back to where Kit waited, his small face streaked with tears.

Squatting on his heels, arms outstretched, Beau waited expectantly for a moment that seemed like a lifetime. He held his breath, afraid to hope, terrified not to. Smiling broadly, Kit rushed into his arms. Beau caught his son and rose, hugging him close, turning around in a circle, propelled by joy.

Still unsure of herself, Savanah stopped just outside the gate and stood shyly, watching the two of them together. Every doubt, every fear, every insecurity was banished from her heart and mind forever when she saw the look-alike expressions of exultation on their faces.

As Beau swung around, he saw her, standing apart, her eyes glistening. He smiled at her and she smiled back. Setting Kit on his feet, he fished into his pocket, closed his fist around something, then opened his arms to her as he had to their son. She came to him, slowly at first, and then she was running down the street, laughing and crying at the same time.

He scooped her up, and Savanah threw her arms around his neck and wrapped her legs around his waist. "Were you really going to just drive off?" she asked, when she'd regained control.

"I thought I'd have to." He kissed her chin and hitched her slight weight more securely into his arms. "What took you so damn long?"

"I don't know," she said honestly.

"I have something of yours." He opened his hand, and her wedding ring glinted in the last rays of sunset. "May I?" he asked. She held up her left hand as answer, and he slipped the simple band onto her third finger. "That's where it belongs. It looks good."

"It feels good."

Love and happiness shone from his eyes as his lips lowered to hers. They were infinitely tender but devastating in their total ravishment. He kissed her as though there were no tomorrow. But both of them knew there was.

Pippy, Jasmine and Doc cheered from the veranda.

"Will you be happy at the hospital in Atlanta?" she asked.

"I see Pippy and Jasmine spilled the beans. I can be happy anywhere as long as we're together. But it's a good offer. I've been thinking, if you're willing, maybe we could buy a house in a small town near there and have the best of both worlds. Could you be happy with that?"

"Absolutely." She didn't even have to consider, she knew. There was only one thing clouding her happiness. "How's your mother going to feel about all of this?"

"My mother will be thrilled to have a grandson at last, she's been harping about it long enough. She's mellowed over the years and despite her failings and past interference, I think she regrets her part in our separation. She was relieved when I told her I was coming here to see if there was anything left for us, so I believe now she truly wants my happiness. That means she'll want you, because you *are* my happiness."

After exchanging a long and reaffirming kiss, they each took one of Kit's hands. The three of them strolled up the walk to the veranda.

"We need a baby-sitter for a couple of days while we work out a few details. Any volunteers?" Beau asked.

"Yeah," Kit exclaimed. "My Mommy and Daddy need to find our new house and stuff." The adventure of it all made the child fidget with excitement.

Pippy and Jasmine exchanged knowing looks. "I reckon we could be bribed," Pippy said.

"Yes, Sister, we surely could. Maybe with that long awaited weddin' in the gazebo."

"It's a deal." Beau squeezed Savanah's hand. "A renewal of our vows would be the perfect way to celebrate our anniversary." He hugged his wife to him, confident of the promise the future held.

At last, he was taking Savanah home.

*   *   *   *   *

SPECIAL EDITION™

Stories of love and life, these powerful
novels are tales that you can identify with—
romances with "something special" added in!

Fall in love with the stories of authors such
as **Nora Roberts, Diana Palmer, Ginna Gray**
and many more of your special favorites—as
well as wonderful new voices!

Special Edition brings you
entertainment for the heart!

SSE-GEN

WAYS TO *UNEXPECTEDLY* MEET MR. RIGHT:

♡ Go out with the sexy-sounding stranger
your daughter secretly set you up with
through a personal ad.

♡ RSVP yes to a wedding invitation—soon
it might be your turn to say "I do!"

♡ Receive a marriage proposal by mail—
from a man you've never met....

These are just a few of the unexpected
ways that written communication
leads to love in Silhouette Yours Truly.

Each month, look for two fast-paced, fun and
flirtatious Yours Truly novels
(with entertaining treats and sneak previews
in the back pages) by some of your favorite
authors—and some who are sure to
become favorites.

YOURS TRULY™:
Love—when you least expect it!

YT-GEN

FIVE UNIQUE SERIES
FOR EVERY WOMAN YOU ARE...

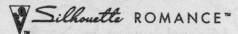

▼ *Silhouette* ROMANCE™

From classic love stories to romantic comedies to emotional heart tuggers, Silhouette Romance is sometimes sweet, sometimes sassy—and always enjoyable! Romance—the way you always knew it could be.

SILHOUETTE® *Desire* ®

Red-hot is what we've got! Sparkling, scintillating, *sensuous* love stories. Once you pick up one you won't be able to put it down...only in Silhouette Desire.

Silhouette SPECIAL EDITION®

Stories of love and life, these powerful novels are tales that you can identify with—romances with "something special" added in! Silhouette Special Edition is entertainment for the heart.

SILHOUETTE·INTIMATE·MOMENTS®

Enter a world where passions run hot and excitement is always high. Dramatic, larger than life and always compelling—Silhouette Intimate Moments provides captivating romance to cherish forever.

▼ SILHOUETTE YOURS TRULY™

A personal ad, a "Dear John" letter, a wedding invitation... Just a few of the ways that written communication unexpectedly leads Miss Unmarried to Mr. "I Do" in Yours Truly novels...in the most fun, fast-paced and flirtatious style!

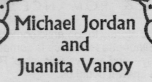

Michael Jordan
and
Juanita Vanoy

At twenty-one, Michael Jordan became an overnight sensation. Women were his only possible weakness. So his mother became his chaperone. "I was really nervous, and my mother became more or less my second eye," he said.

Juanita Vanoy, a loan officer at a Chicago bank, was a mother's dream. They began a love affair and had a son in 1988. It wasn't until their son was almost a year old that Jordan announced he was ready to get married. The couple flew with friends to Las Vegas. "Why do I trust her?" Jordan asks rhetorically of Juanita. "Because she's so like my mother."

In Vegas, Jordan balked. "I told Juanita I was afraid that when the preacher asked if there was anyone who objected to the marriage, too many hands would go up. I didn't trust my buddies because they saw it as the start of another stage of my life, and they knew that would limit them. So I said, 'If you want to do it, let's do it now.' We'd both had a few drinks, we'd been gambling and losing—this was like our bachelor night. That's how we got married at 3:30 a.m. in a wedding chapel. I did say that years from now we could do a church wedding. And that's what Juanita is banking on."

B-JORDAN